Crimson Prophecies

Crypt V

Blood Oath

KILTRON

Copyright © 2022 by Dan Harrington

All rights reserved.

No part of this publication may be produced, distributed, or transmitted in any form or by any means, including photocopying, recording, or other electronic or mechanical methods, without the prior written permission of the author, except in the case of brief quotations embodied in critical reviews and certain other non-commercial uses permitted by copyright law.

ISBN
(Paperback) 9798841158776
(eBook) 9781005624798
(Hardcover) 9798841159094

I dedicate this to everyone that has read my stories and offered their criticisms;
And have told me to get my editorial shit together.
I'm praised for my story telling, how great it is.
That I'm an above average writer, good enough to get the job done, but my edit skills suck! True story, Bro!

Crimson Prophecies
Blood Myth
Blood Shadows
Blood Lovers
Blood Lust
Blood Oath
Sanguine Slave (Upcoming)
Bloody Sorrow (Upcoming)

Wolf Moon Chronicles with Nightwolf
New Moon Rise
New Moon Feast
Runaway Moon
Witch Moon
Winter's Wolf Moon
Siren's Moon (Upcoming)
Lazarus Moon (Upcoming)

Acknowledgements

A big special thanks to **Janice Saunders** for our little talks at work and the blasts of poking fun at costumers and the dumb shit people do. I love my job. Glad to have you reading my crap and making edit suggestions that *needed* change in this series.

Of course, big thanks to **Jay Crudge** who likes to poke the bear. My reviewer likes the characters, although he does wish certain ones would just die already, lol! Love yah man!

Thank you, **Various Methods**, for the lyrics to the song **Fall** that grace these pages. The song makes so much sense for the events in this series. Can't wait till the new album is out!

Thanks to **Derek Fehr** and his wife **Melissa Fehr** for buying my stuff and reading it. Also, for encouraging me to press on and not to give a fuck about what people think. "Write whatever *you* like" is the Quote. So, I write whatever I feel like.

Thank you **Maria Brink** of **In This Moment** for the music you produce. Love and health to you.

Another special thank you to **Meg Myers.** Darlin, when I need crazy, I listen to your music. It drives me to dark places I really need to go. Hugs girlie!

High five to **September Mourning** who's music continues to inspire me to push forward. I read your posts and your quotes fill me with a need to keep going when the chips are down. Thank you, September. May the deep running peace be with you! Metal forever! *Raises fist and yells*

Now, **Zora** of **Blackbriar.** Your siren's voice helps to zone me out and write like the madman that I am. Peace, Love, and Eternity to you and the band.

Blessed be the Universe!

Author's Note!

I make apologies to all the readers of this book ahead of time. Good luck reading this novella of the series. This one is full of sorrow and heartache. There is so much pain and agony the melancholy of this roller coaster ride will have you in tears the whole way through. Sadows and her friends must deal with the loss of a loved one. Everyone's stress levels are through the roof and go beyond limits. Friendship bonds will be, forever changed, and not just for the better either.
Change is coming!
Sadows wants revenge!
Her sadness knows no bounds as this adventure takes place and you, the readers will hate me or love the story told, or both.
I will still love the fans of my works even if they are pissed at me.
Hope you enjoy the story regardless. Even if Sadows is in a dark place.
Later my bitches!

*"Kiltron has done it again!
He has brought on the pain and suffering!
Give me more!"*
-Jay Crudge

"In the mind of madness there is only the agony of maggots devouring the last bits of sanity!"
-Various Methods

*"I Can't believe the author killed off Zivan and is making Sadows suffer like this!
Bring it on!"*
-Melissa Fehr

*"What the Hell just happened?
Has Kiltron just lost his mind writing this?"*
-Jarrett Wright

*"Brilliantly done!
We get to see what Sadows is really, made of, at last!"*
-Hell & Malfunction

*"Kiltron never disappoints!
The emotions displayed is so realistically surreal!"*
-Derek Fehr

Mourning

Sadows laid in her bed curled in a fetal position. She has been there for days now, sobbing her heart out. Tears stained her burning cheeks. Her heartache was beyond anything she has ever experienced thus far in life. She no longer wanted to live. The love of her life was now gone.

My Zivan!

Sobs wracked her body. Two other women held her in their arms. Chandra cradled Sadows' head to her bosom and whispered assurances.

Sitri held the day walker from behind and cried along with her friend. The demoness would kiss Sadows' shoulder and rub her legs.

Chandra and Sitri looked at one another with tear-streaked gazes. They had taken turns laying down with their friend. But her suffering did not ease in the least. When Sadows would cry herself to sleep she then awoke later throughout the night screaming Zivan's name. She was reliving what had happened to him each night. She normally never slept except those few times with her man.

Sadows' body suddenly stopped shaking and she dosed slowly off to sleep with slight whimpers.

Sitri looked at Chandra. She mouthed the words; *I will stay with her.*

Chandra nodded and kissed Sitri's hand.

Thank you, the voodoo priestess mouthed back. Sitri teared up again. This was the first time the queen of New Orleans has shown affection toward the lust demon. Sitri basked in it for a moment. Then cuddled into Sadows and held her until she too fell asleep.

Chandra left the room. She allowed herself to be, held in the arms of her voodoo Baron.

Samedi kissed his queen gently and she accepted him whole heartedly. She needed him. His comfort. Chandra began to cry.

"Easy Cher. I'm here my love," Samedi whispered into her hair. Her arms went around his neck.

"I'm sorry that I was incapable of protecting him..." he tried to say.

"Shh! It wasn't your fault, Mon," Chandra whispered. She kissed him gently.

"Oh Cher," he whispered back into her mouth.

"Love me Samedi. Then love Sitri," she murmured and leaned into him.

Samedi pick his queen up into his arms and carried her to another room where they would make love.

Chandra clung to him as if she were a frightened child.

Still, no one would sleep well. They have not slept in days since Zivan's disappearance. The horror that happened to him imprinted into their minds. Just as was the aftermath. What Aila did to end the onslaught of the vamp horde.

It would haunt them until the end of their days.

Sorrow

"Zivan."

She ran. Her legs felt sluggish as she reached for his outstretched hand. Felt like swimming in a dream. The harder she tried to reach the love of her life... the further he seemed to stray away from her.

Panic wrapped its disassembling arms around her. Sadows fought with everything she had. Every fibre of her being, raged against the pull that prevented her from reaching Zivan.

What was this force that held her back? What was this weird white light that made the environment look like a strange void? Yet she still could not reach her man. Why?

Zivan stood still and beckoned to her. Sadows heart sored. Anxiety overwhelmed her emotions. Her body shook non-stop. The shakes felt as if they would take her apart.

Sadows became desperate now. She shouted out to him. Her voice sounded hollow. There was no echo in this bright white void.

"Zivan. Please wait for me. I love you."

Words that became flat and dull. Why did her voice sound so strange?

This stress was too much to bear.

"Zivan."

Again, she ran to him and again he was, pulled away or dragged down by heaviness.

He said something. The day walker could not understand his words. Could barely hear them. She focused on his lush mouth.

"I love you, Sadows," *he spoke with a broad smile.*

Sadows' heart skipped a beat. She smiled back and knew it melted his heart. He loved her smile. He blew a kiss to Sadows. She made a motion of catching it and brought her hands to her own lips. Then blew a kiss back. He caught it and kissed his own hands.

Sadows suddenly found herself getting closer to Zivan. Elation filled her. A joy that she had not known in sometime swelled within her chest. Her breathing laboured. The closer she got to him the more excited she became. Could not wait to feel his touch. To kiss his full lips.

So, close now. Sadows reached out and strained her muscles.

Almost, there!

Zivan smiled brightly.

A shadow passed. A pale clawed hand came around Zivan's throat. A long nail slashed his throat. Silver Eyes glared into Sadows' red orbs that teared blood. Fangs drank from the love of her life. In a blur of motion Zivan was gone.

Sadows screamed.

Sadows awoke screaming Zivan's name. She thrashed upon the bed. Sitri gripped onto her friend.

"Sadows, calm down, please," Sitri urged.

"I want my Zivan back," Sadows yelled as loud as she could.

Her hands were placed on Sitri's face. Frantic eyes gazed into the demonesses.

"Love me," Sadows begged and kissed Sitri. The lust demon pulled away. Sadows eyes turned red like boiling blood. The day walking vampire grew angry and attacked Sitri. Her fangs sank into the demoness' throat. Sadows drank deeply.

"Bos Moi, girlie," Chandra yelled, as her and Samedi burst into the bedroom. They pulled Sadows away.

Sadows panted and watched the blood drip from Sitri's neck.

The vampire mourned. Tears of blood streaked her cheeks.

"I'm sorry Sitri. I... didn't mean to hurt you," she sobbed out. Sadows broke down.

"I'm alright Sadows," Sitri assured her friend.

Then threw up a stream of vomit all over the demoness. Sitri stunned just laid there.

Chandra gasped. The voodoo queen instinctively held back her friend's hair.

Sadows puked again on Sitri. The demoness let out a huff of breath.

"Just let it out," Sitri groaned in embarrassment.

When Sadows finished she felt weak and tired. She still had tears in her eyes.

"I'm so sorry Sitri. I have ruined everything," Sadows sobbed and gagged.

"Come Cher. We get you clean up," Samedi said as he picked her up and carried her to the bathtub. Chandra and Sitri followed.

"Thank you, Samedi," Sadows said as she kissed his cheek and hugged him.

"It is no trouble Cher," he replied with a faint smile.

"I will get you cleaned up, girlie," Chandra offered.

Sadows nodded.

"Samedi. Help Sitri get cleaned up, please. And have fun," Chandra winked.

Samedi chuckled and took Sitri by the hand. They left the room.

Chandra helped strip Sadows down, then took her own clothes off. She turned on the water and the water showered down until it warmed. The two women showered together and washed themselves clean.

Afterward, Chandra helped Sadows to another bedroom with clean sheets. The two of them laid down and soon fell asleep in each others' arms. This was the only way Sadows had any sort of peace. She had to lay embraced with one or both of her friends. She could never be alone ever again. All she ever felt now was sorrow.

Fairy Dance

Keena danced about in a glade somewhere in a forest. In a part of the world where she liked to be. The fairy was doing what faeries normally do. Staying out of trouble. As it is well known. Faeries never cause trouble of any sort. Right? Wrong!

Keena danced in her usual manner. She hummed, which meant she was about to sing.

She twirled around and leaped about with splayed arms in the air.

"I love, I love;
I need to fuck!"

Her words were musical in the morning breeze. She touched the leaves of the trees and smelled the flower blossoms. She inhaled deeply. Her dark mane writhed like a living being. The strains caressed the grass and weeds. The tree trunks bark seemed to pulse to her touch. Keena rubbed up against one of the trees and moaned.

I need to get laid, she thought to herself. *I want a nice virgin boy to ravage.*

Her thoughts grew a little darker. She felt a desperation. An idea came to her, and the fairy girl giggled. Then disappeared only to reappear somewhere else.

Another part of the world where it was noon hour. Here there were... *Boys,* she could take advantage of. Good thing she was not human. She was about to break so many of their laws. She grinned madly. This was a high school full of young virgin boys primed and ready for her to have sex with. This faerie was about to rock the worlds of all the boys she could this day.

There were estranged looks passed her way but also looks of interest. Keena decided she did not care who knew what she was. Wings released from her back, and she flew up in the air in front of everyone.

There was shock and awe as people stared at her. Keena sent out dark mist. The mist formed into small balls of darkness that glowed faintly. Four of the orbs went out to seek their virgin victims.

Keena came back to the ground. She fluttered her wings. Black fairy dust caught by the breeze. All the students around became coated in it.

They soon had smiles and trance like looks in their eyes.

Keena began to dance about.

I am Keena, Keena!
A nymph you want to use.
Abuse me, abuse me!
I will love you.

The dark nymph pointed to students that grinned in anticipation. She put her two fingers by her chin and stuck out her tongue at a girl who blushed. Keena giggled and gave the girl a light kiss on her lips. The girl swooned and fell to the ground.

Let me lick between your thighs;
Let our ties bind.
Beat that dick in me;
Pump me full of need.

Keena grabbed the crotch of a young boy who rose to the occasion. The faerie unzipped his pants and stroked him until he passed out during ejaculation. Keena threw her head back with a hearty laugh. She spun around and leaped in the air. Wings carried her up then she landed in front of a girl with glasses. She held her books close to her bosom.

These words I sing to you;
I will make sweet love to you.
For it is true that I want to lick you;
And finger fuck you too.

Keena's hand went under the girl's shirt. The books tumbled to the ground. The faerie tweaked the girl's nipples. She gasped in pleasure. A breast bared, and Keena's mouth wrapped around the nipple and sucked gently. This girl also swooned. She then fell to the ground unconscious.

Hello, little boy;
Come, play with me.
I am eager to please;
Spill your seed in my belly.

Keena turned to mist and reformed in front a boy. It happened so fast. His pants around his ankles and the dark nymph's mouth sucked his penis. He fell to his knees and closed his eyes. He was out like a light. Still, he filled Keena's mouth with what she wanted.

This naughty faerie wanted to do good things in a bad way to these young adults. This little pervert liked to ravage the underaged teens every so often. In the human world such things were illegal. Keena cared less about such things. She was a dark nymph, and she could do as she pleased. She had true power and not a damn human on the planet could stop her. This is what her kind did. Faeries were known to rape men of all ages. Have for well over a million years, now. But back in ancient times it happened to be, called seducing. Male humans were breeding cattle. Keena liked it that way. She enjoyed taking advantage of young humans. Especially these teenagers. It was so much fun.

    Keena suddenly paused in her dance. Four students surrounded in black mist came toward her. Three boys and a girl. All virgins. Now, the fun would begin.

House Cleaning

Lorca and Zoe cleaned the house in the Mississippi swamp just outside of New Orleans. It was Chandra's grandmother's house. They were cleaning and filling the pantry with food and what not for Sadows, Sitri, and Chandra's return.

The two women could not wait to reunite with their friends. This would be a better place for Sadows to mourn and recuperate.

Then they could go in search of Zivan. Zoe was sure that her brother was still alive. Her and Lorca would set off when it was time to find him.

Aila had sent out word of his disappearance to all her packs. If anyone could pick up that dirty vamp's trail, it would be her.

The dark nymph Keena was out there somewhere looking also, but she may not be so dependable. She was too random. Did things when her mind might remember the task at hand. The blasted faerie easily distracted in a bi-polar way. For all anyone knew the nymph already knew where Zivan was and did not tell anyone to suit her amusement.

Fuck that bitch! She's a cunt! Zoe thought in statements of fact. *But She is still hot and a great lay.* She shook her head with a wane smile.

"Hey, hon. You, okay?" Lorca asked in concern.

Zoe must have had that look she expressed when lost in her thoughts.

"Yah, sort of. I mean…" Zoe sighed deeply.

Lorca hugged her wife.

"I love you and we are going to find him," the vampire turned fae assured.

"I know my love," Zoe replied and leaned into the love of her life.

"Hon. We will find him. He must still be alive. I know what we saw… but… that bitch vamp wanted him for something. She wants us to believe he is dead to demoralize us. She…" Lorca stopped. A realization overcame her. She had a suspicion and whispered it to her mate.

"Do you think so?" Zoe responded.

Lorca nodded.

Zoe thought it over and had to agree.

"We shall do a ton of shopping before the others get here. How about we call it a night then," Zoe suggested heavily.

Lorca smiled. She had naughty thoughts of her own brewing in her mind.

"I'm down for some sexy time, baby," her voice panted as she kissed Zoe's full lips. House cleaning would have to wait. Tonight, both women would be in the throes of passion.

Flings in the Woods

Keena brought the four students into the woods. Her woods. Faerie woods. Sparks of light drifted about like puffs of pollen. Faeries flittered like fireflies, weaving through the tree boughs.

Keena amused and joyful at the sight. She smiled broadly and spun around with her arms stretched out. The song began.

I twirl and I whirl;
I hump and I fuck.
Baby!
I will lick and suck on you;
Explode in my mouth so I can swallow you.

Keena danced around the tree trunks. Her dark luminescent wings glowed. Her mist sprinkles sprayed into the air and fell back down like a rainfall. The dark nymph rubbed herself. she made her thighs wet in anticipation. Her scent filled the air only to arouse the students she brought with her. Her voice mesmerized every living creature close by. The students watched in awe and wonderment.

Keena! Keena!
Your dark faerie bitch!
Keena! Keena!
I will be your sexy witch!

The dark nymph grabbed one of the boys and shoved his face to her crotch.

"Lick my dirty faerie pussy you, filthy man," she breathed heatedly.

She moaned as the boy's wet tongue tasted her juices. Keena moaned louder as she bucked her hips into the boy's face. She gripped his long dark hair. His dark eyes closed in ecstasy. The faerie exploded her pleasure upon him.

"Yes! Drink my creamy essence. It will keep you hard and full of seed for me," she said between gasping breaths.

The boy drank then fell on the ground. Keena mounted him and rode like she was upon a horse. His hands squeezed her petite ass.

"Oh, my virgin boy," Keena panted.

He let out a groan of pleasure that made him gasp for air. The dark nymph enjoyed the spray of his ejaculation inside her. It only heightened her own pleasure. She then kissed the boy deeply.

> *You cannot get enough of me;*
> *I want every drop of your seed.*
> *I will make you bleed;*
> *As my dark mist seeps into thee.*

Keena sang into the boy's mouth. Kissed his lips. Dark mist seep within him. Keena had laid claim.

She stood and beckoned another one of the boys to her. He was a dark-skinned lad. Dark like night. the moonlight absorbed into him. Keena liked the boy very much.

She turned around and slapped her ass. She leaned forward and looked seductively at the midnight skinned student.

"Take me from behind," her voice was alluring.

The boy walked up behind her. He vaguely wondered how they all had no clothes on. Also wondered where they all were.

He entered within the faerie and groaned pleasantly. He pumped his hips some more before he threw his head back as he came.

"Keep fucking pounding me," Keena yelled out. Her passions rising. Faerie mist sprayed upon this new boy. He let out a deep groan.

Keena moved away quickly only to place his member in her mouth.

"Oh baby, I'm Cumming!" he grunted.

The dark nymph took all he gave.

"Mm! Yummy in my tummy!" Keena stated. The boy collapsed on the ground as black mist enveloped him. Another victim claimed.

Keena smiled as she observed the last boy and the girl. She had an idea.

"Come to me my children," the faerie beckoned.

Both students walked toward her. Keena kissed both on their lips. The girl laid down on the ground. The dark nymph kissed the girl's private spot. A lick here. a lick there. The girl was a brunette with hazel eyes bright as a sandy beach.

"Feels good!" the girl breathed.

Then Keena sucked on the final boy. He groaned deeply. He was hard and ready.

"Fuck her!" Keena whispered in his ear.

The dark nymph guided his penis to the other girl's wet loins. The girl kissed him. Keena pushed on the boy's ass cheeks. His penis penetrated deeply. He grunted. The girl squealed a moan as pain and pleasure sparked within her. The girl held the boy close to her.

"Make a baby with her," Keena whispered again.

"Yes!" the girl screamed out her orgasm, "Impregnate me!"

The boy released his pleasure. The boy and girl kept kissing each other. Tongues wrapped and twisted. Saliva dripped and smeared.

Keena managed to wiggle herself between them. She kissed the girl gently.

"Watch as he fucks me." She whispered to the girl. The girl watched as the boy slipped inside Keena's love hole, his rhythm picked up the pack. The faerie moaned her pleasure in his ear.

"Release inside me like the others did," Keena begged as convulsions of pleasure wracked her body.

I am in heat!
I am in heat!
I need to breed!
I am in heat!
I am in heat!
Stick your dick in me!

Keena whisper sung to the new couple. She kissed them lovingly. She like them the best. She would not claim them as she did the other two boys. But she did plan to continue her fun with the two boys. She smiled pleasantly. Her mind was clear of cobwebs. She let the couple continue to love her and kiss her and pump into her. Just for this moment the dark nymph wanted to be loved by them. Their emotions were felt. Their feelings were strong for her. They were willingly falling in love with her and each other. The faerie liked that. Wanted that. She knew a baby would be born within the girl. Her magic could sense the conception happening. This made her happy.

Keena! Keena!
Your dark faerie bitch!
Keena! Keena!
I will be your sexy witch!

They both lamented Keena's name. It brought immense pleasure to the dark nymph's ears.

Keena left the couple to love one another. Black mist surrounded them, and they transported to a glade in another forest.

Keena had more plans with the two boys she wanted to ravage some more.

Is it wrong of me to have sex with these two boys? They are young. Not children but not adults either. I, myself am ancient. Does it really matter that a being like me takes advantage of these underaged boys? Do I even care?

Keena thought for moments. She paced around from boy to boy.

"Nah! They want to fuck me. It's alright!" Keena laughed heartedly. Her song picked up and the boys were ready for more.

Love me like a whore;
I am the only woman you adore.
I will make sure you are, never bored;
With me you shall always score.

It did not end there. Keena, the dark nymph took both boys at once. She enjoyed the love they put into her. Until they could not give more, and they were asleep.

The faerie frowned. She gently cradled the flaccid penises in her small hands. She sighed deeply in disappointment.

"I want more," she said to herself quietly.

Then a smile broadened on her tiny features. She knew were to get more. More virgins to feast upon. This time she wanted to be, taken by three or four at a time. Her twisted mind only fell further into madness. She needed her dark desires sated.

Searching Thoughts

Malcolm thought back on the fight him and his wife had. She was right. He had to except the decisions of his children.

Malcolm blamed Sadows for the disappearance and possible, death of his son. Blamed her because she was a vampire. The worst kind in his mind. *A Day Walker!*

She could not die by the sun's rays. Silver didn't hurt her. He could try beheading her. Or fire even. But he had this dreadful feeling that even that would not work.

Malcolm demanded that their children would no longer be around these vamp lovers anymore. He wanted them out of his children's lives.

His wife had eyed him with narrowed brows.

"Clearly you do not understand the relationships our children are in. These are not flings, Malcolm. Our daughter is married to a beautiful woman. Our son was with a beautiful girl that protected him," Her voice had begun to rise.

Malcolm tried to speak but she interrupted him with a raised hand.

"Now, you will not interfere with the relationships of our children. I mean it," she said with a glare, "You will take the squad and find our son, alive or dead. But you will find him." Her voice quivered. Tears welled up in her eyes.

"Bring my son home."

Malcolm held his wife then. He kissed her forehead then her lips.

Later that night they made love and held one another. They whispered and kissed.

"...that girl is in bad shape. She cries non-stop, day and night. She loves Zivan more than anything. Her and her friends will try to find him," she murmured.

They just held each other until they fell asleep.

Malcolm thought about this as him and his team flew in a helicopter over a wooded area in the Yukon. They would be at an old log cabin in minutes. There a plan formulated to find his son and hunt down the vamp that took him.

A Mother's Love

A Mother's love can be an immensely powerful emotion. When Lucile went to Toronto to meet Aila, the wreckage she saw was daunting. There were construction crews cleaning up the area and knowing the she-wolf, there were already plans to rebuild.

The day walking vampire girl Sadows covered in blood and tears wailed Zivan's name as if that would bring him back to her.

She knew Zivan's blood stained the day walker's face. This news almost broke her. Then Sadows did something both amazing and disturbing. She took Zivan's blood and scared it like a tattoo into her left arm. It turned black but gave a crimson glow in the light. Forever branding his name.

Aila frowned deeply. This kind of reaction was bad. Sadows had been, broken and no one knew if even Sadows realized who she was anymore. This kind of sorrow was more than destructive, it was also bordered line suicidal.

"I want my Zivan back," Sadows cried in agony.

Lucile broke down then. She went to the vampire girl and hugged her tight and sobbed with her.

Aila had contacted Lucile. Told her she must be in Toronto right away.

Zoe and Lorca met with her. Told her what had happened to her son. Zoe told her mom everything.

Now, Lucile held the girl who loved her son. Zivan loved this vampire girl. She wondered if her husband knew yet. She would travel to Sweden to inform him.

"Mom! Lorca and I will search for Zivan. He must be alive. That silver-eyed vamp has been stalking him. Her name is Aaruhi..." Zoe did not get to complete her sentence.

"...Daughter of God!" Lucile finished.

"That's right!" Lorca agreed.

"So, this creature, truly exists? A silver-eyed immortal?" Zoe's mom asked.

"Yes... but... ah... she somehow turned into a vamp. From what we understand these silver-eyed ones can't turn into vamps or werewolves," Zoe explained.

Her mother nodded. She still held Sadows in her arms. The day walker had fallen asleep. Lucile looked at the girl fondly. Her heart went out to Sadows, and an acceptance overcame Lucile. She kissed the vampire's forehead to show her blessing.

"I will take care of her now while you, Zoe, and Lorca make a plan," Sitri said quietly.

Lucile watched as the demoness gently held Sadows in her arms and laid down.

A demon that showed such affection to her friends was mind blowing. Lucile understood all too well. She would do whatever it took to retrieve her son back from the clutches of an evil vamp. One should not underestimate the love of a *Mother.*

Travel Arrangements

The two women were trying to figure out how to travel back to New Orleans.

"Fuck Mon, how we gonna get Sadows to my house?" Chandra asked with her arms folded.

"We could ask Keena," Samedi suggested.

"Yah right, Mon," Chandra spat with sarcasm.

"We transport her by using a coffin," Sitri said.

The voodoo Baron and voodoo Queen looked at the lust demon in surprise.

"What? I know it sounds a little cliché, but we have the cash to do this. I will stay in the coffin with her to keep her calm," Sitri assured.

"I batcha would, Mon," the voodoo priestess voiced in a sardonic tone.

Samedi raised his eyebrows at his queen. He knew where this would lead to.

"I would not take advantage of her like that," Sitri raised her voice. She looked to Samedi for support.

"Cher! I believe Sitri can manage this," the voodoo Baron said.

"Don't you defend this slutty demon whore. You damn well know she will try something on Sadows now that Zivan is gone," Chandra said heatedly.

"Fuck you, Chandra," Sitri blurted out, "how dare you think I would try to seduce my best friend. I wouldn't do that! I love her *as* my *friend!*" Sitri said in a whiny voice.

"Calm, Cher. Chandra, give Sitri a chance to do this. You know she does not see Sadows and Zivan in such a way as she once did," Samedi said in honesty.

"Samedi. She is a hypersexual deviant. She might..."

"Hush, Cher. Trust!" he said and kissed Chandra's lush lips.

"You know how to work me, mon. Fine! Sitri, get everything together and then we will leave," Chandra said and glared at the demoness.

"Already done!" Sitri said with a smile. The demoness kissed Chandra's mouth.

"Thank you. Love you," Sitri breathed into the voodoo priestess' mouth. Then turned away.

Chandra narrowed her brows. Then placed hands upon her hips.

"Dat girl, Mon," she said and shook her dreaded and braided head.

"Dat girl is on da ball," Samedi whispered in his queen's ear.

Chandra could not help but smile. Samedi was right. Sitri had it together. Sitri was a huge slut, a whore even. Nymphomaniac. Chandra felt pride for her friend. Yes! Sitri was her friend now. The voodoo priestess admired the demoness.

"Samedi. You think Sitri could... Never mind," Chandra finished.

"Yes!" Samedi said and kissed Chandra. She did not know it then but in the future the answer would slap her in the face.

Coffin Love

Chandra and Samedi used their magic together to keep Sadows asleep for the trip. They exerted a large amount of magic to calm their friend until she finally passed out. To be honest if Sitri had not helped it may not be, achieved. The lust demon impressed the voodoo queen once again. The girl has progressed.

Chandra cleared her throat and pointed her finger at Sitri.

"Now girlie, you behave yourself, Mon," she scolded.

"I'm not going to do anything, Chandra. Sadows is…" Sitri whined.

"Oh, shut up!" Chandra snapped.

"Easy Cher," Samedi consoled.

"Yah! He slammed me earlier," Sitri said with a snobby attitude.

"Bos Moi, bitch!" Chandra gritted her teeth in annoyance.

"I would fuck you, but you're such a bitchy prude that is so... damn hateful of me. Am I that repulsive to you?" Sitri grew annoyed at herself now.

"Why you..." Chandra sputtered.

"Stop, Cher." Samedi said and gripped Chandra's wrist to prevent her from slapping the demoness.

"I knew you wanted me," Sitri said with a sly smile and hopped into the coffin with Sadows' sleeping form.

Sitri cuddled into the day walker. She then stuck her tongue out at her voodoo queen.

Chandra glared. If Samedi had not have put his arms around her waist she would have pounced on the demoness.

Samedi closed the coffin lid. He took a deep breath. When he exhaled his shoulders slumped.

"Cher. My love. It was nice having these few days of peace between the two of you. Can we just continue thinking of our friend in need?" he said sadly.

"Samedi I..." Chandra tried but let her words hang.

"I love you, Cher. Sitri loves you." Chandra furrowed her brows at the mention of Sitri's feels toward her.

"Bos Moi, Mon. You lucky I love you, Baron," the voodoo queen said.

"I know Cher. One day you may end up loving Sitri too," he said and kissed one of the loves of his life.

Chandra embraced her Baron. Her anchor. Her tether to the voodoo goddess.

They moved the coffin into a Hurst of all things. This seemed ridiculous. They were taking a private jet that Aila sent. Was there a need for Sadows to travel in such a manner? Maybe! She may have been able to be on the plane itself but in transition to and from the plane would make things difficult. Sadows condition in public would be problematic. To face the matter head on, Chandra and her friends were not exactly normal human beings.

The coffin loaded onto the jet and Chandra and Samedi sat in their seats waiting for take off. Chandra genuinely believed things would be better for Sadows in New Orleans.

Chandra just hoped that Sitri would behave herself. The Whore! This was the beginning of the voodoo queen's jealousy.

Sitri cuddled with Sadows in the confines of the soft padding in the coffin. She felt the plane lift off and closed her eyes. When she opened them

Sadows' crimson orbs glowed! The demoness started, and her own eyes went dark.

Suddenly Sadows' lips meet Sitri's. The day walker tried to force her tongue into the lust demon's mouth. Sitri pulled away.

"Do you not love me?" Sadows asked.

"Of course, I love you. Just... not in that way," Sitri replied uncomfortably.

"I'm sorry, Sitri. I... don't know what came over me," Sadows whined and then began to sob.

The demoness held her friend. The glow went out from the vampire's eyes. She turned around to let herself be, held from behind. Sitri held her friend tightly and kissed her hair.

"Thank you for being here for me," Sadows said between sobs.

"Always!" Sitri assured.

There was a time Sitri wanted both Sadows and Zivan. To be the creamy filling between them would have been heaven to her. Now, things are so different. Sitri loves her friends too much to betray their love. Sitri cried with Sadows. Cried for Zivan. She would do everything in her power to help her best friend.

Sadows began to fall asleep again. Her murmuring words faded off.

"I want my Zivan back!"

Keena's Betrayal

Keena, the dark nymph was more than content. She had found more virgin victims to play with. Forty boys she laid with. The faerie was happy in her little maddened world.

Keena moved her arms and legs about as if she were making a snow angel. She giggled herself. so, gay, and free, covered in a sticky substance. Keena licked off her fingers.

"Mm! Yummy! You boys taste so good in my tummy!" the dark nymph praised in joy.

Then she frowned. She looked about at all the unconscious bodies.

"Aw! Why is everyone out cold," the faerie pouted.

She stood and rubbed the bodily fluids over herself. Keena reveled in it. The faerie stretched and absorbed the sticky substance into her body.

Keena's thighs were sore. She did not mind. Sex with one girl and forty-four boys. Keena was still hungry for more.

A spin and twirl. A whirl and a leap. Wings sprouted out from her back and took flight in the air. She sighed with a smile.

Then a thought struck her as if she were, slapped in the face. There was this yearning to do what her thoughts told her to do.

Yes! She must visit a friend. It must be, done. Maniacal laughter burst from her lungs.

"I shall do it!" Keena yelled out to the woods.

She danced in the air black mist sprayed like a rain.

"My pretties for me. Sleep until I return and lust for you," she voiced like a mantra.

In a blink Keena disappeared. Her reappearance was a cavern deep underground. Bookshelves lined the walls. A figure stood by with a book in their hands.

"Hello, Ti' Nish' Hah," Keena said joyfully and skipped over to the ancient vampire.

"Good evening dark nymph. What do I own the pleasure of your visit?" the ancient vamp asked.

"To tell you that I was just Cum covered by many boys," the faerie said proudly with her chin up.

The vampire chuckled.

"Were they younger than they should have been?"

Keena nodded with a toothy smile.

"I seem to remember in the old days when you and I would do such things to fourteen years of age. Virgins. We would fuck them, and I would drink them. Then turn them," the vampire said with a smile.

"Oh, I remember," Keena said excitedly, "that's why you have to come with me, now," Keena said hurriedly and gripped the ancient's hand.

They were gone in a poof of black mist.

Chasing Memories

She heard rumours of vampires here in London. Heard of a hunter and a girl who slayed them.

This woman however was tracking them. She was not worried about vampires; they were easy to dispose.

This woman knew who the girl was she tracked. The girl was also a vampire. A day walker. This was no creature of the night. This girl was immune to sunlight.

Now the man the girl traveled with was unknown to her. He was a vampire hunter. But it would not take her long to find out his name.

As for the city she was in, it was a large city. One of the largest in Europe. A real shithole in her mind. Most cities were cesspools. Paris, like most cities became disease ridden at one point by the Black Plague that killed millions across Europe and Asia. Fools had not realized that it was an insect called a flea that lived in the fur of black *rats. These rats came from Asia during the Mongolian invasions.*

Rats.

Vermin.

Must exterminate.

Just like vampires. Vermin! They too must perish. Destroy the vermin.

Such a delightful thought on her part. Still... she was a vampire herself. But she felt different somehow. Her hunger was gone. It only took a small amount of blood to nourish her anymore. To think that she was wasting away in her prison overcome with the thirst. Then she drank from the girl. At first, she thought she had died. She did not. She was reborn. Made whole once again.

She had drunk from Sadows. The day walker wanted to save her or at the very least give her a peaceful death. No! She had become something more and was happier now. This was why she must find Sadows and tell her of the miracle the day walker had performed.

She awoke from her sleep. She opened the drapes to the night sky that was full of city lights. What a glory that cities have become. Now, this was truly modern. A transit system that took you to every part of the city for a small fee. Events everyday of the week all year round. This city did not sleep in the downtown area. It was alive with millions of people. The clubs were a great hunting ground to feast and kill other vamps.

She was here for one reason and one reason only. There was a YouTube video of a boy and girl who fell or leaped from the tallest tower in the city. That girl had grown wings to fly and saved the boy.

The woman turned from the window and went into the bathroom. There, a vamp wrapped in silver chain panted. The woman smiled. Her fangs extracted.

"Hm! How tasty shall you be little vampy vamp?" her voice was menacing. She bit into its flesh and drank deeply.

I cannot wait until our reunion my dear, Sadows.

The Den

Here and now is where Malcom and his team had found a new vampire den. It was a long shot, but he hoped this was one of the dens that belonged to that silver-eyed bitch vamp who took his son.

My Son!

Malcom struggled with his emotions. He hated them. They clouded one's judgement and the decisions he had to make. It was important that his head stayed clear for this raid. His team had to survive this. If red hot rage overcame him the mission was lost, and they would all die.

Zivan had to still be alive. This cunt had a plan. She may turn him sometime soon. No matter what, a father's worse fear realized.

Control yourself! Don't fuck this mission up. Malcom's thoughts became dark and filled with mourning. Tears held in check. He would focus on the task at hand.

Malcom gave the signal to move in. Brock took the lead as he always did. Stacy right behind him to cover the rear. They were a team and effective. They had each other's back and now that they were a couple, it would be more effective. They had already proven it.

Brock's weapon was a mobile mini gun or something akin to it. It was a plasma type weapon. Its rounds were like sending bursts of sunshine up a vamp's ass. It is a very efficient weapon for mid to close range.

Stacy had a flamethrower slash assault rifle. Fire was just as deadly as silver to vampires and this woman knew how to be a wrecking machine.

Everyone wore night vision goggles and had UV lights on their helmets and weapons.

"We have vamp action people. Look alive," Brock yelled into his commlink and commenced firing. Plasma rounds tore apart and burned through vamps like a paper shredder.

Stacy let loose her flames into every room along the way as they went deeper into the den. This empty warehouse had tunnels beneath it. Malcom and his team started the clean sweep.

It was a den of that silver-eyed witch for sure. These vamps were feral monsters like all the others she has made.

The squad systematically exterminated every vamp they came across. When all was done here the den would be; destroyed like all the others.

It did not take long to finish the job. Seemed odd that there were too few vamps in a large den as this. Malcom did not like this. Was this a small den to throw them off track so he could not find his son?

"Sir! I found an escape tunnel," a squad member reported.

"Show me where, Sasha," Malcom commanded.

He came to a concrete tunnel with a grate. They both went into a tunnel system.

"This is newly constructed," Malcom said more to himself.

Sasha was suddenly pushed back into the grate.

Malcom tried to spin around but his arms ended pinned behind him. Pain laced up to his shoulders.

"Well hello Zivan's daddy," a malicious voice sounded in his ear. Lips kissed his neck. "I wonder if you taste as good as your son," Aaruhi's voice breathed. Her tongue licked the nape of his neck. Her hand gripped his crotch.

"Mm! Feels nice to me. I should take you also," Laughter sounded. It was more like the giggle of a malevolent child who enjoyed torturing animals in the forest. Fangs sank gently in and for a moment Malcom felt ecstasy. He moaned in pleasure.

The silver-eyed vamp gazed at Sasha with a nasty quirky smile while she drank.

"The bitch is here! Move to my position now," she shouted into her commlink. In a matter of seconds Stacy and Brock showed up. The others close behind.

Aaruhi stood behind Malcom. He was now on his knees with a glazed look about him. The silver-eyed vamp made a point to expose his neck to show that she had fed from him. Blood dripped from her grinning mouth.

"Zivan tastes so much better, but I'm willing to ravage the father also," she laughed out.

"B... burn her," Malcom said weakly.

Stacy stepped forward without hesitation and let loose a fury of flames into the tunnel.

Brock shot rounds high which hit the ceiling behind Malcom.

The vamp was gone. They knew she was unharmed. At least Malcom was safe.

There was no sign of Zivan. Wherever Aaruhi had him it was a damn good hideout.

"God, that bitch is such a cunt," Stacy gritted.

Brock nodded his agreement.

"We will get her one day," Brock said calmly. His fists clenched tightly.

Stacy touched his arm and he relaxed. She smiled. Brock saw only sunshine in that smile and could not wait to get home to taste those lips upon his own mouth.

Sasha helped Malcom to his feet. He held his neck. It still bled a little bit.

"We set the charges. Starting here," he said and placed a charge above the grate tunnel.

This place would be nothing but a pile of melted slag.

Hold Me

Zoe and Lorca continued their clean up duties in Chandra's Bayou home. They were close to finishing. They only had to clean the last remnants.

Everything cleaned inside and outside. Light bulbs changed. Everything worked and the two women even bought items such as new appliances and food.

The last bit was done. Laundry finished washed and dried. Lorca was in the middle of putting clothes away and making all the beds in the house.

They did not touch Grandma Chandra's room. They did not have the heart to do so. It still smelled like her, and they were afraid to take that away.

Zoe washed the rest of the dishes and put them in a dish rack. She would dry them with a towel when it was full then continued to wash more.

She let music play on her phone. The list was large. Just into so much different music. This was upbeat. This music could work to anyway you wished. The band was September Mourning. Song was *Kill This Love.*

You're a storm out in the ocean and you've come for me.
No air inside these lungs and now I'm drowning deep.
The light drains from my eyes, hope is so hard to keep.
And I'm lost to the sea.

Zoe liked this song. It reflected current events. How strange. Then a verse came and hit her like a ton of bricks. This song did reflect what happened with Zivan and how Sadows was feeling.

In my heart.
You left your blade.
To cut me to pieces.
It's so hard to kill this love.
Are we ever gonna kill this love?
No, you're never gonna kill this love!
No, I'm never gonna kill this love!
No, it's never gonna die!

Zoe frowned and tapped the screen to change to another song. She sighed and dried her hands then the phone. She reacted without thinking and got it wet. She continued to wash the last bit of silverware while a new song played. This one was a mournful bit of lyrics also. Zoe shook her head. It was another song she liked. By Blackbriar. Mortal Remains was the name of the song.

I am digging deeper into the dark sand.
Cold and wet earth in my bare hands.
A desperate undertaking, it is all I have left.
I cannot live with this unbearable pain in my chest.

Zoe took a deep breath and leaned on the sink. She squinted her eyes shut tightly. She just turned her phone off. No more music. Tears came to her eyes.

Arms wrapped around her waist. Zoe gripped those hands and held on to the comforting embrace her wife gave.

"Oh, baby. We will sort this out, my love," Lorca whispered in her ear.

"We must find my brother and make that bitch pay. I will..." Zoe did not want to finish that sentence. Could not allow anger and grief to cloud her judgement. "Just hold me!"

Lorca kissed her wife's pale brown neck. It was not as pale anymore. Zoe's skin had gotten darker during summer. Zivan by far was the darkest of skin in the family. She envied her brother for that.

Zoe arched her back and pushed her ass into Lorca's pelvis. The other woman moaned softly with an intake of breath.

"Oh, I love that ass of yours," Lorca said and grabbed Zoe by her butt cheeks.

Zoe spun around to face her lover.

"Make love to me," Zoe pleaded as she leaned against the countertop.

No more words spoken. There were just kisses and moans of pleasure.

Save Me

Lacy walked the streets alone. They were empty tonight. Far from silent with the construction of the ruined quarter that was happening twenty-four-seven. The company had gotten special permission to work at all hours of the day and night.

All the ash removed, and the ground leveled. Concrete poured. Building had begun so soon. The Mayor of Toronto wasted no time in restructuring. There was a giant sign showing the next Highrise. The Sapphire. This building made of blue tinted glass of over a hundred floors. It would have a large sapphire like jewel atop that would light up the night.

Lacy smiled. Now that was a place, she wanted to live one day.

She moved on toward her condominium. She was tired and missed the man she had known so briefly.

Where are you love of my life? I have never felt this way about anyone, before!

Her thoughts were so deep that she did not see them in front of her until one of them spoke in a dark grunted voice.

Lacy froze in fear as it shot up her spine and made the hairs stand on the back of her neck.

She looked around her and realized they had surrounded her. There were five men or what appeared to be men.

"I see London. I see Paris. I'm going to get into your underpants," one of the men said with malicious intent.

She suddenly knew what would happen to her. It dawned on her what they were.

Vampires!

They were going to rape and drink her dry. Lacy began to shake. Her hands held to her chest.

"Tevin. Please save me," She whispered softly like a prayer.

Oni looked down upon the city of Toronto from the C.N. Tower. Beside her stood Tevin, her demon lover. Oni struggled with these new emotions she was having. Unsure whether to embrace them or deny them. She was a demon slayer after, all.

The demon male wrapped his strong muscled arms around her. Oni gasped. Loved the feel of him pressed against her body. To think that she has always been more into women than men.

He kissed her shoulder. The silver-eyed samurai moaned pleasantly.

"Tevin," she breathed.

"Oni," he breathed, but she could sense that he needed to talk about something that was important to him.

"Hm, yes!" she replied.

"Lacy, the woman I told you about…" he let his words hang a moment. Not sure if he wanted to continue or to wait for Oni's reply.

"Yes, I remember. You said you both have a bond from having sex, right?" she asked.

Tevin nodded. He opened his mouth to speak. The silver-eyed samurai hushed him with her lips.

"I'm okay with it. Even if you want her too, which mind you I know you do," she scolded playfully.

"I don't want to choose between the two of you. I want to be with both of you," Tevin said with guilt.

Oni gazed at him deeply. She saw his struggle and the emotional pain it caused.

"Alright! I'm okay with it. You think she will like me?" Oni asked with sincerity.

Tevin could not believe his ears. This wonderful woman was willing to accept another person in their relationship. He was surprised.

"I only accept this as long as she doesn't hurt you," Oni stressed.

Tevin's eyes went wide suddenly.

"She calls," he breathed.

He grabbed onto Oni. He felt the tethers wrap around him. Oni felt them also. They felt gentle but beckoned with urgency. Then they were gone from the rooftop.

The vamps moved in upon Lacy. Their laughter filled her ears with dread. She shivered. They were going to do horrid things to her.

The wind picked up and a whooshing sounded. A roar of rage heard, and a vamp was torn to pieces.

A beautiful woman with silver hair and silver eyes appeared. Her silver blade made short work of vamps as their limps sliced away from their bodies. The final vamp, the one who threatened Lacy, crushed to a pulp.

"T... Tevin," Lacy cried out and ran to her man.

He embraced her in his arms and held the girl he barely knew close.

"I said your name and you came. I'm so happy you came to save me," Lacy sobbed. Her tears flowed freely. Lacy cried for what seemed like a long while.

When she had stopped crying, Tevin lowered his lips to hers and they kissed long and deeply. Lacy moaned.

"Oh, my love," she breathed out. "Love me." It was demanding. She would have him.

Lacy gazed longingly at Oni.

"Tevin is she, our girlfriend?" she asked curiously.

Oni laughed and it soon turned into a giggle.

"Oh, Tevin. I like her already," Oni managed to say when her laughter calmed.

"You are so beautiful," Lacy said in awe.

Oni gripped the girl's chin. The silver-eyed samurai kissed the other woman's lips.

"I look forward to loving you," Oni breathed in the other woman's mouth.

Old Friendship

Back out into the wilderness they went. It has been over a thousand years since the ancient vampire has been outdoors. She marveled at how the world has changed.

Keena used her magic to keep them invisible from prying eyes. Their little tour was brief but Ti' Nish' Hah was in awe of how large and different a city had become. They light up the night like nothing ever seen before.

Soon, the two women came upon a glade where sleeping boys lay.

"My gift to you and their sexual prowess is exactly what you need," Keena said with an accented lilt.

The ancient vampire gave the dark nymph a sideways glance. She knew the faerie was from the Misty Isles. Most times Keena would have a Scottish Gaelic accent or a Welsh one. The woman was a faerie, and they could use any accent and speak any language they pleased. Keena was devious and cunning. The danger she possessed was beyond measure. The dark nymph was mad. All faeries had one type of madness, but Keena exceeded all forms of it. Still, it did not change how the vampire felt about her. Ti' Nish' Hah loved her either way.

"I thank you for the feast, my love," the ancient vampire spoke. She kissed the dark nymph's dark lips with such a passion that her heartbeat had skipped like a schoolgirl.

Ti' Nish' Hah walked among the sleeping forms. She felt a tethering tug. Something she has not felt in over a million years. It was strong.

There! That young boy.

A pleasurable pain hit Ti' Nish' Hah's pelvis. There was no mistaking it. He was the one. All she would need is his consent and…

He awoke and looked the ancient vampire in the eye. His gaze was of wonder. His eyes dilated until they were almost black. Only a sliver of green could be, seen. His carrot top mane was long and wavy.

"You are beautiful," he blurted out.

"Why thank you!" she stated with emotion. Emotion she had not felt in so long.

Her desire for this boy grew and made her loins wet. It was not just for sex but also for companionship.

She observed his naked form. Her hands reached out and gently touched his flesh. Tingling sparks jolted between them. She gasped and he groaned.

"By the way. I saved the last virgin for you to take. I knew he would be the perfect match for you," Keena whispered in the vampire's ear.

The dark nymph's tongue licked an earlobe then nibbled it. Ti' Nish' Hah groaned softly.

The male boy was hard and inviting.

"Are you willing to be turned by me?" she asked him.

"Aye! With all me heart, love," he said thickly.

Irish! Mm! Finally, a mate!

She then mounted his manhood. He grunted in pleasure as she moaned hers. She was not into drinking blood unless she had to or was to turn someone. Her sustenance was a man's sperm. She fed off it.

Ti' Nish' Hah bit into the flesh of the boy's neck and drank until he was almost empty of his life essence. His eyes grew diminished and drooped. Then the ancient vampire took a clawed nail and inserted it into her nipple. She gasped in pleasure as the pain sparked her orgasm. She brought the boy's lips to her breast like a mother would her newborn child. Soon as his lips met, he began to suckle which brought such ecstasy to the vampire. Her Quim convulsed. The boy grew stronger with his change. He bucked his hips. He grunted loudly as he released himself uncontrollably.

Ti' Nish' Hah was in awe of how he released so much into her. She must have it all. With such speed her mouth was around his penis, and she sucked back the rest of his semen. She had never known a man could produce so much before. She liked that very much.

The boy laid there panting. He was so tired.

"Sleep my darling," Ti' Nish' Hah murmured into his mouth. She kissed him lightly and he fell asleep.

The vampire looked about at all the other sleeping forms. She had planned on fucking all of them but changed her mind. She still needed to feed. However, she would suck the sperm out them instead.

Keena watched with a smile. The vampire would be indebted to her for what she planned next. Being the dirty girl that the dark nymph was she began to masturbate near her vampire lover where she went to feed.

A faerie must get off, you know!

Michael's Search

His search had led him here of all places. Middle of the ocean. An area known as the Abyss. Deep in its depths was the mirror shard. He could sense its faint presence.

How was he to solve this dilemma? He could hold his breath for an extremely long time, but he still was not sure he could survive the pressure that far down. He was not sure if he could drown or not. He was a silver-eyed immortal. The only person he could think of that could kill an immortal was that Alpha woman, Aila. The Sun Shaman. She was a scary piece of work. Michael was sure her flames could destroy about anything.

A thought just occurred to him. What if the Alpha werewolf's flames could counter act his brother Lucy's? Could she cure him? It was worth a try. He knew where to find her. She was Sámi.

The angel shuddered at the thought of her flames burning him.

Wings flapped gently to keep him hovered in the air. Music could be, heard, it was faint. Then he saw a figure in the water. Michael flew down toward them. The angel stayed out of striking range of the creature. It was what he suspected. The woman before him was a siren. A type of mermaid with the ability to enthrall men to their doom. Her voice was pleasurable to his ears. It did not allure him to her. The kiss of God has protected him from such power.

"You seek the mirror shard," she said matter of fact.

"What gives you such a notion?" He asked.

"Why else would you hover over the very spot it lays," she threw back.

Michael narrowed his brows.

"I can retrieve it for you," she said, "but you have to do something for me first."

Michael took a moment to think it over. He would hear what she had to say.

"Alright then. Out with it."

The Bayou

They had reached their destination at last. Samedi had driven the Ali-Wang through the swamp to Chandra's childhood home. The home of her grandmother. The thought of her voudon grandmother made Chandra tear up. She wiped them away then glanced to her Voudon Baron. He noticed but pretended not to. Chandra smiled slightly. She loved that man.

Emotions toiled within her. She was jealous of him and Sitri's love for one another. She was not so sure how to feel about the demoness' feelings toward her anymore. The time in the alley confused the voudon queen. She was turned on by Sitri and did not understand why. She had never been into women in that way before. Although she has only been with few men in her life. There was Samedi and two one nightstands and they were not worth a damn. She just was not into those men.

She glanced in Samedi's direction again longingly.

He is the man for me! She thought privately.

"I love you, Samedi," she said abruptly.

He gazed lovingly at her.

"I love you too, Cher," he replied. His smile was bright and genuine. He loved her. She felt it radiate from him. It felt like a warm embrace that caressed her lush curves. Chandra's breath quickened. She wanted him here and now.

Her lips suddenly met his in an enthusiastic kiss that ignited a blaze in her heart.

Samedi let go of the throttle and powered down the boat. He kissed his queen back with all the emotions he had. His tongue caressed hers gently.

"Oh, Samedi. Love me," Chandra breathed.

"Fixin' to," he said with a smile.

Chandra giggled and kissed him again.

Their love making was slow and tender. They took their time. This was perfect here in the Ali-Wang, in the swamps. It felt like home.

The feel of him inside and against her was paradise. Chandra never wanted this to end.

Then energy began to twine around them. Green electrical like flames slowly enveloped them.

"Oh, Chandra," Samedi groaned as he sunk into his queen slowly.

"Oh, Samedi," Chandra moaned as her hips rose into him.

They both climaxed together. Heat flooded throughout their bodies. It felt like a merging of two souls becoming one. Chandra kept her legs wrapped around his waist and she gripped his shoulders. Samedi embraced her and did not want to let go. They laid there for over an hour just holding each other. Lovers. Mates. A Queen and her Baron. Together.

They were once again riding through the swamp. This time Chandra drove the Ali-Wang. A content smile upon her ebony features. Her green orbs took in her home with a new spiritual awakening.

They reached the dock of her home. Zoe and Lorca waited for them there.

The two women squealed in glee when Chandra stepped off the boat. She hugged them. They had her between them, as always. They did the same to Samedi. To be with her friends again felt great. A happy moment deserved.

It was Zoe and Lorca who brought the coffin ashore, and they put it in a glade. Chandra thought it would be better for Sadows to awaken to the sights of nature.

Chandra opened the coffin, and the two occupants were… well one was still asleep.

"Bos Moi, girlie," Chandra gasped, "Wat yah do dat?"

Sadows was flicking one of Sitri's nipples. One of the demoness' breasts was bare.

"See how it bounces. It reminds me of a door stopper. The ones that make that funny sound," Sadows was so intent on her friend's nipple.

"Come outta dare, girlie," Chandra admonished gently.

Sadows climbed out with a smirk. This was a good sign. Chandra hoped.

The day walker looked about and took a breath of fresh swamp air. She stretched her limbs and let Zoe and Lorca hug her. She did not want them to let go. Tears formed and she sobbed quietly as possible in their embrace.

Chandra leaned into the coffin to wake the demoness. Without a thought she flicked a nipple, and it did exactly what Sadows said.

"Bos Moi, Cher," Samedi blurted and slapped his forehead. He began to laugh. Chandra went red faced in embarrassment.

"Shut up!" Chandra mumbled.

The Queen of New Orleans brushed hair away from Sitri's face.

"Rest easy, girlie," she said under her breath and gave a faint smile.

Sitri's eyes opened slowly, and the demoness yawned. Chandra pulled away swiftly.

"Chandra?" Sitri said tiredly. "Are we here?"

The lust demon sat up then noticed that Sadows was missing.

"Where's Sadows? Is she alright?" Sitri began to panic.

"She's fine, girlie. You such a panic case," Chandra grumbled and walked away.

"What's up with her?" Sitri asked as she looked at Samedi.

He had a bright smile on his dark features. Sitri loved that smile. Made her heart melt. Then she realized that a breast was showing.

"Wait! Chandra nothing happened with Sadows. I promise," Sitri shouted out.

"We know, Cher," Samedi assured her.

He wrapped an arm around her shoulders, and they walked to the house.

Voodoo Past Love

Chandra and Samedi went into the hut together. This would be their first time. They would no longer be virgins. Baron and Queen.

They have grown up together. Been childhood friends. Learned the voudon ways from Granmè – Grandma Chandra. They learned Creole as their language. Erzulie their Goddess.

They held hands as they knelt before one another. This was their first kiss as lips met. Tongues clumsy with passion played. It was still sweet and heated them up. Chandra laid down and Samedi went on top. She helped guild him into her. It stung as he thrusted his way in. Roughly.

"I'm sorry, Cher. You awrite?" he fretted.

When he saw the blood between her thighs, panic seized him.

"Samedi, it is awrite. Dis what happens when a woman loses her virginity," she assured him. Her hips rose into him as her hands held his face. Their lips met again, and they kissed deeply.

Chandra gasped. She felt a pressure building up inside her. She began to shake and shiver. Her head thrown back. Her release was unlike anything she had ever felt before. She felt something else hit inside her at the same time. She liked it very much.

Samedi groaned loudly as he spent his sperm within Chandra. They held onto each other for dear life. Their love making did not last long but it was intense and the memory of it would last until their dying breaths.

They laid in each other's arms for the night. Before morning they would make love again. This time it lasted longer, and they teased one another, explored one another. Ever since then every time Chandra was with Samedi it was so much like that night. It was like magic. Love.

"See Cher, dat was how we fell in love. I have always loved Chandra. You have been the second woman that I have been with," Samedi said after finishing his story. Sitri sat with a smile.

"So, beautiful," the demoness said.

"What of that Spanish slut I caught you kissing in the alley?" Chandra spat out harshly.

"First, it was a horrible kiss. Second, she noticed dat you were dare and acted like it was awrite," Samedi shot back.

He took a deep breath.

"I never liked dat bitch. There was only you. You spurned me, Cher. I never stopped loving you," he confessed.

Chandra stood up. A smirk appeared on her lush mouth.

"Sitri. It is time to go to bed," the voodoo queen said.

"Okay," Sitri said without argument.

Chandra held her hand and they went into her grandmother's bedroom.

Samedi sat there with a bright smile.

Like Sisters

Sadows cried in the arms of Zoe and Lorca. They lay on either side of her. Zoe cried along with the day walker. Lorca had tears in her eyes. She did her best to be strong for them.

"I'm so sorry Zoe, for not being able to protect Zivan," she sobbed out.

Oh, Hon! It's not your fault. We all tried to protect Zivan," Zoe tried to hush her friend.

Sadows clung fiercely to both women. She had missed them dearly. The day walker then snuggled deep as she could into Zoe. Zivan's sister was the closest tie to him, now.

"You and Lorca are my sisters, right?" Sadows sniffled out.

"Of course, we are!" Lorca stated and squeezed her arms around Sadows' waist.

"We love you sis!" Zoe whispered and kissed the vampire's forehead.

"I love you both," Sadows said tiredly. She soon fell asleep as did Lorca and Zoe. Their comfort kept Sadows calmer. It also helped them in return. A moment of rest. Action would be taken to search for Zivan. It was important that Sadows led this charge. For Zivan's sake.

Zoe's thoughts were in turmoil before she slept. Lorca's touch soothed her.

Everything shall be alright, my love, Lorca's thoughts gently intruded into her wife's mind.

Ever since they were able to commune this way, they practiced every chance they got. It has become their lifeline. They were discovering new abilities. This one however connected them on a deeper level and Zoe was grateful for it. She loved her wife with all her heart.

Thank you, my love. For always being here for me, Zoe sent her message back.

They both leaned over Sadows' sleeping form and kissed. They both snuggled back into Sadows.

Comfort!

Together!

Loving!

Sisters!

Return Trouble

Lucile walked with Clare to the ancient vampire's lair. Lucile stressed over the news her husband had just given her. Him and his team had encountered that silver-eyed cunt of a vamp. That bitch had fed from Malcom. First her son, now her husband. The silver-eyed witch was playing with them. All this had just put her in a piss poor mood.

If only she could be out on the hunt. What Lucile would do to get her hands on that vamp.

Lucile started when Clare placed a hand on her shoulder.

"Ma'am, I'm sure your son will be, found. This ancient vamp can help us with Aaruhi," Clare spoke like a robot.

Talk about living the part as a techno-witch. Such strange behavior. One would almost think the woman were an android.

That thought lightened her mood. Somewhat.

"Thank you," Lucile replied and patted the other woman's hand.

They continued and went into the chamber. There Aila was in the vampire's den. Flames surrounded the she-wolf.

"Keena," she roared. The door to the room blew open and became melted slag against the opposite wall.

There it was. The emotion Lucile wanted to see in Clare. She was pale faced in fear and disbelief. From what she understood about the vampire's prison was that no force on earth could blast that door open. With the technology and the magic wards, not even a nuke could blast it apart. Clare had seen to it herself. The power Aila just exhibited was scary on a whole new level. She was after all the Sun Shaman.

The she-wolf walked out to greet them.

"Lucile, Clare. Looks like we need to find a way to keep that damn dark nymph from getting into our facilities," she commanded.

"What happen?" Lucile asked.

"The little cunt teleported in and took the vamp who knows where. This will be a whole lot of trouble," Aila gritted her teeth. Heat still radiated from her.

She turned into the doorway and stood there musing to herself.

The she-wolf blinked then a smirk appeared. She let her canines show.

Keena had reappeared with the ancient vampire and a boy.

"Well, I will explain everything to Aila. She will understand," the faerie explained.

Course, Keena was not looking where she was going and walked right into Aila's nude form.

"My, what nice, muscled breasts you have," Keena said stunned.

The dark nymph gazed up and frowned at the look the she-wolf gave her.

"'Faeries never cause trouble.' 'Faeries never get into trouble whatsoever.' The damnable quotes spouted from your filthy mouth you, fucking slutty whore," Aila raged. Flames flickered in her already amber eyes.

Keena shrunk away from a finger that pointed into her chest.

"Yay! You are mad at me. I'm sorry about that. I figured Ti' Nish' Hah needed air. Hey, she made a friend, see," Keena displayed with a show of her hands.

"Oh, I see that. How old is the boy by chance?" Aila asked with a snarl.

"Fifteen, I think," Keena said in a weak voice.

"Fifteen," the she-wolf yelled. "Have you lost your mind? He is underage you dumb fuck. He must have family. You kidnapped him. Someone will be looking for him, like his GOD DAMN school. Maybe." There was no end to Aila's fury, and the dark nymph flinched away from the Alpha. The heat from her burned Keena's skin. The ancient vampire was worried and embraced her newly made ward.

"Do you hate me, now?" Keena asked with tears in her eyes. "Please don't hate me. I love you Aila. I'm sorry," the faerie begged as she went to her knees with her hands laced together in a fist.

Aila knelt before her long-time friend.

"Do not interfere with what I am doing ever again!" she stated harshly.

"O...okay! Can we have sex now?" Keena stuttered out.

Aila grimaced. Then she gave a deep sigh. Aila leaned in.

"Perhaps later," the she-wolf whispered.

The Dark Fey shivered. Keena wanted to feel the Alpha's power inside her. It made her wet in anticipation.

"Now Lucile. Go ask the ancient vamp your questions," Aila demanded.

Lucile wasted no time in doing so.

"Do you have any idea how we could find the silver-eyed vamp, Aaruhi?"

Ti' Nish' Hah narrowed her brows. This was a dangerous thing to ask.

"What I know is that you must stay away from that insane bitch. She was once a silver-eyed Immortal. They are enormously powerful and the cause of our fall. Aaruhi is an unknown to me. The Crimson Queen changed her herself, just as I was," the vampire said.

"I've met one of these Immortals. Her name is Oni," the she-wolf said.

"You have met with Oni of the silver blade? It is said that all the immortals are siblings. That they are not in agreement with the subjugation of humanity. Oni is who you want to track Aaruhi. There is a long hatred between them that goes back before Aaruhi turned. The Silver Blade knows how to kill about every creature that there ever is, was, or ever will be. It is her talent," Ti' Nish' Hah said. This information was good although it still did not reveal where they could find the vamp.

"She has taken my son for an obscure reason. We are certain he is alive. She needs him for something," Lucile said.

"I wonder. She may want to turn him after torturing him. She loves to do that. She..." the ancient paused. "No! She might be trying to have a baby. To see if it is possible to do so. She is known for doing experiments with her vampire powers. She has made different breeds in the past," the vampire revealed.

Lucile gasped. That would mean that her son was being... She dared not think it.

"What is your family lineage?" Ti' Nish' Hah asked.

"Tepes," Keena spoke up.

The ancient vampire gasped.

"That cannot be. That Dacian family was, exterminated long ago," the vampire said with conviction.

"No! The Crimson Queen protected that family line. I saw to it myself," Keena revealed.

"Keena! Do you know where to find Zivan?" Aila asked carefully. It had just dawned on her that the faerie might have that knowledge. She knew too much about everything.

"Well! I must go now. Love you all," she said with cheer. Her whole demeanor had changed, and she stuck out her tongue. Then disappeared in a blink of black mist.

"Keena!" Aila raged.

That answered everyone's question. Keena knew more about everything that was going on than she ever let on.

"I'm going to burn that fucking bitch to ash."
Aila would be true to her word.

Tumbling Down

Alice!
    My name isn't Alice!
    Down the rabbit hole you go.
    She fell for what seemed like forever ago. At first the shock of falling scared her to no end.
    She felt like Alice. She just hoped not to land in Wonderland. That would be weird and creepy.
    She felt calm now as she fell in this deep dark hole. It was like one of those comedy movies, but this did not feel very funny. It was lonely. Depressing.
    Was that a song playing?

You let me in.
I climbed up inside.
Wanted me to see.
Places where you hide.

She felt almost hidden as she continued to descend. Hair whipped up like a national flag on a windy day.

> *Everything in here.*
> *Is, painted black.*
> *I think that you, knew.*
> *I'd never find my way back.*

It was so dark here. Nothing to see. There was no way back. Fear started to grip her again. Cold claws of dread in her chest.

> *How I wanted.*
> *To loose it all.*
> *I was never so, ready to…*
> *Fall.*

There was a slight pause before the words 'Fall' where said. It felt like it took such a long time before the song continued.

> *Ready to fall.*
> *Ready to fall.*
> *Ready to fall.*

But she was not ready to fall. Hated this feeling. If only she could fly. That would be better.

It became so easy.
Adapting to this.
Felt like the safest place.
In something so, dangerous.

Do you think? This falling thing is dangerous. She sure as shit did not feel safe for a single moment. There was no adapting to this situation. Not super easy or barely an inconvenience.

I started to believe.
What I knew was never true.
Everything I did to myself.
Cause, I couldn't hurt you.

Believe in what? This is not happening. Was there someone trying to hurt her? Why the fuck was this song playing anyway?

How I wanted.
To loose it all.
I was never so, ready to...
Fall.

This verse played again. The chorus, right? Then...

Ready to fall.
Ready to fall.
Ready to fall.

This played again. She heard this song before somewhere. She knew it was, well received. She liked it.

Sank a little deeper.
In your demise.
You did it in little bits.
So, I'd never realize.

She was sinking alright. Not really a word to use when one was falling down the rabbit hole so to speak. She was going to realize her demise a split second before dying when hitting bottom.

You made that something.
Just to puncture through.
Made me feel I couldn't live.
Unless I had been fucken you.

Fucking!
   There was something she had missed doing with the one she loved but he was gone now. Taken! She needed him back.

How I wanted.
To loose it all.
I was never so, ready to...
Fall.

Again!
      She suddenly felt tired. Wanted to sleep but it would never come.

Ready to fall.
Ready to fall.
Ready to fall.

Still was not ready to fall. Then came the outro of the song to end it.

Ahhh...ahhh...ahhhhhhh.
Ahhh...ahhh...ahhhhhhh.
Ahhh...ahhh...ahhhhhhh.
Ahhh...ahhh...ahhhhhhh.
Ahhh...ahhh...ahhhhhhh.
Ahhh...ahhh...ahhhhhhh.

The song ended with such a mournful groaning cry. A lonesome moaning of anguished pain that tore at the heartstrings. She gripped her chest and cried. Her tears floated upward because of the speed of the descent.

Then he was there. Reaching out to her. Eyes went wide in surprise, and she stretched out to reach as much as possible.

"Zivan," she shouted in such joy.

They held hands and then soon embraced. Wings released from her back and then they were flying at such a speed upward. When they reached the top of the rabbit hole. Their lips met in a long-lost kiss.

His smile was a thing of beauty. Her heart melted. Then the smile was gone and replaced by a gash in his throat. Blood splattered her face.

"No! Not my Zivan," she screamed.

Silver eyes appeared and a fanged mouth bit into Zivan. Then he was gone, and malevolent laughter sounded in the distance.

Once again, she fell through the rabbit hole to continue her spiraling descent.

Sadows awoke like she had times before, screaming for her lost love.

"Bring back my Zivan," her scream awoke everyone in the house. Both Zoe and Lorca were flung against the walls.

Sitri was the first to get into the room before Chandra or Samedi.

"Sadows. I'm here," the demoness shouted.

Sitri gripped the day walker's face between her hands.

"We are here for you, Sadows," Sitri said urgently and hugged her friend.

"Oh, Sitri. It was horrible," Sadows sobbed out.

"I know it was. But you are safe now here in the Bayou," the lust demon cried with her friend.

"Bos Moi, Mon," Chandra breathed in relief.

Samedi held his queen. Chandra leaned into his arms.

"Sitri. We should take her downstairs to Maw Maw's room. I think we should spend the rest of the night there together," she suggested.

Everyone agreed.

Zoe and Lorca picked themselves off floor. They all went downstairs to Grandmother Chandra's room. This would be a safe space for Sadows. It is enchanted and hopefully the nightmares would not persist so long as she slept there.

Everyone managed to fit on the bed. It was a large California bed after all. They all snuggled together. Sadows in the middle. Sitri on one side, Chandra on the other. Samedi held Chandra while Lorca held Sitri, and Zoe held her wife.

Suddenly, Sadows began to giggle. She tried to stifle it but kept laughing.

"What is it, Mon?" Chandra asked.

"Well…" Sadows paused a moment thinking whether she should comment or not. "It's kind, of weird you see, with all of us here and me in the middle with my pale skin. It's like I'm the creamy filling of an Oreo cookie," she finished.

Everyone began to laugh hysterically.

"Oh, Cher. That's a good one, Mon," Samedi said between fits of laughter.

Sitri looked at Sadows quizzically.

"I don't get it," Sitri said, "and what's an Oreo cookie?"

"What? Are you me kidding girlie?" Chandra asked.

The demoness shook her head.

"Look at you, Mon. Skin pink like the inner folds of me vag…" Chandra slapped her hand over her mouth.

Everyone roared in laughter. Sitri gave a smirk.

"Someone has been thinking dirty thoughts about me," Sitri accused playfully.

More laughter erupted.

"She got you good, Cher," Samedi teased.

"Bos Moi, girlie. You set me up. I know you did. Don't you deny it?" Chandra accused.

"Maybe!" she said and licked Sadows ear.

"Ewe! No wet Willies," Sadows giggled out.

"I was just licking the creamy filling of the Oreo cookie. Now, it's time for chocolate yumminess," Sitri laughed out.

"Oh, snap girl," Zoe said and high fived the lust demon.

"You go girl," Lorca praised.

More laughter sounded throughout the room. This was good. All this joy and happiness. This is what the day walker needed.

Chandra, not done yet continued the conversion.

"So, Sitri. You know all our virginity loss stories. Tell us yours," Chandra demanded with a smirk.

"Darling, you realize how old I am, right? It's been thousands of years and to be honest. I don't even remember ever losing it," she said with a look of bewilderment.

"Wait! Seriously," Sadows asked tiredly.

Sitri nodded.

"I've been with so many people I've utterly lost count if I could count that high to begin with. Doesn't matter. I'm a slut and proud of it. I love and fuck to my hearts content. I enjoy it and am not ashamed of it," the demoness cemented her pride about it.

Chandra gave a wane smile. She liked that answer and did not understand why, but one day she would.

"I feel so loved," Sadows said as she drifted off to sleep again.

Chandra snuggled into the vampire girl. Sitri waited a while then kissed Chandra's cheek.

Sleep well my Queen," she whispered.

Chandra was not asleep yet. Heat rose to her cheeks. She squeezed Samedi's hand, and he responded. A sign of acceptance. Change was coming and friendship bonds along with it.

Sitri Loves

Everyone was awake, bright eyed and bushy tailed. Coffee made. A good Kenyan brand. Breakfast made and everyone ate their fill.

"Sadows, would you like to go into the swamp today with us girls?" Chandra asked.

"Okay! Sounds like a plan. Will we get to see those fish like people?" Sadows wondered.

"Maybe, Cher," the voodoo queen replied with a smile.

"This will be fun," Sitri said with excitement.

"You stay here with Samedi," Chandra said too quickly.

Sitri frowned in disappointment.

"Someone has to guard our home," Chandra said with a wink then walked away.

Sitri clued in and smiled.

Thank you, my queen, the demoness thought to herself.

"Enjoy yourselves," Lorca chuckled.

"Don't do anything I wouldn't do," Zoe yelled out and laughed.

"Come, Cher," Samedi said as he held her hand. Sitri followed him back into the house. They went upstairs to one of the bedrooms.

Sitri could not wait to be in the throes of passion with this hunk of a man.

They undressed and soon were on the bed. Samedi caressed her soft silky skin. She burned with desire.

"Love me completely, Samedi?" Sitri begged.

"Mais Yeah – but yes," he replied with excitement.

He then slid in between her folds. She raised her hips to meet his thrust. The demoness moaned in pleasure.

"Oh, Samedi. Fuck me with that magic dick of yours," Sitri panted out and threw her head back as an orgasm struck her hard.

"Oh Cher," he moaned into her mouth.

"I want to have your baby, too," she screamed out.

It felt so good to be beneath him. He pumped into her, and those orgasms continued. They kept coming non-stop. She did not want them to stop. He was her magic man. An ebony god that made her feel alive with love and desires. He feed her and she fed him back.

He turned her over to do it doggie style. She would let him do anything to her. He knew how she liked it and she liked it everyway possible.

Samedi thrusted hard against her ass cheeks. The grip on her hips tightened as he released himself within.

Sitri rubbed her clit to heighten her pleasure.

They laid down to take a breather. Sweat glistened their bodies.

"I love you, Samedi," the demoness breathed.

"I love you too, Cher," he whispered back and kissed her. Their hands moved together then entwined.

"You think that the three of us could ever be together and marry?" Sitri asked.

"I believe so, Cher. Chandra just needs time to process her emotions. The thought of being with another woman has never occurred to her before, much less a demoness hottie such as yourself," he teased.

Sitri giggled. She enjoyed the voodoo Baron's company. They could talk about anything. She was comfortable around him. He loved and desired her. Made her feel like a goddess at times. He was such a beautiful man. His heart was true. He also loved Chandra and that also made Sitri happy.

Suddenly Sitri began to cry. She sobbed uncontrollably.

"Cher. What is wrong?" he asked in concern.

"You and Chandra will grow old and die on me some day," she balled out.

"Easy, Cher. It is awrite. Do no fret about it. We are here now, and we will always be here," he explained and touched her breast over the heart.

He embraced her and when she stopped crying, he asked, "better, Cher?"

She nodded.

Their mouths met and they made sweet love for a second round.

Pacing and Fretting

Keena paced in her cave. A place where no one could ever find her. There was one way in and out. You teleported in like she did and only Keena knew the location.

She was troubled by her own thoughts. Did she really know where Zivan was? Sometimes her mind would darken and grow hazy. Scattered fragments like shattered glass moved like lightning in her mind. Memories and images of times long gone and what may have just happened.

The faerie was disturbed by this and Aila was angry with her. Keena was afraid for the first time in her life. Could the Alpha burn her to ash? Fafnir once loved her right? Or was it just her desires for him that played tricks on her?

OH, what I would do to have that wolf man between my creamy thighs, she thought as she touched herself. She would masturbate on it to clear her head. After her relief Keena was no closer to being clear headed at all. She became more confused. Anxiety was a crushing weight in her chest. The Dark Fey could have sworn she heard something. Jumpy as all hell. She had to leave. There was something that must be, done.

Keena disappeared in a blink of black mist.

A shadowy figure walked into Keena's little room. She was a regal figure. Dark. Her skin ebony as onyx. Eyes just as black with a shine to them. Her dark hair was a writhing shadow.

Well, my dark daughter. What has you so spooked? What of your light half sisters? I will catch you and you shall explain why you murdered your brother. Do not make me summon you child. These thoughts were dark and full of loathing.

The Outing

Chandra drove the Ali-Wang into the swamp. They made a brief stop to see the so called 'Fish people' that Sadows wanted to see.

The boat drifted upon the still waters. Everyone was silent and waited.

One of the creatures surfaced. They rose out of the water and leaned into the boat.

"Wow! They are so amazing," Sadows marveled.

"True dat, girlie," Chandra commented.

Sadows could not help herself and hugged the fish person.

"It's a girl and she have big boobs, so, cool," the day walker squealed in joy.

"Bos Moi, Mon," Chandra swore and slapped her head.

"Take a pic of us," Sadows said with a grin.

Zoe took out her phone and snapped a shot of the day walker with a big tongue hanging grin and her making the peace sign.

The fish creature went back into the water, but its eyes peeked out above the surface to watch.

The Ali-Wang drifted for a time before Chandra started it up again and drove it down one of the waterways.

Next stop, New Orleans. Time to shop and try to have fun. A night out on the town. Besides, Chandra had a place they could stay at for the night.

Soon, the girls were in the city and Sadows looked around like a child in a candy store. She had forgotten how wonderful it was to be here.

They went into a dress shop. They all tried on colourful sundresses.

"Damn, girl. You look yummy in that dress. I want to get under it and have my way with you," Lorca teased Zoe.

"Mm! Please do, hon. Ravish me like the tart that I am," Zoe laughed out.

Chandra wore a long gown twined with orange, yellow, and a multitude of greens. She was stunning, like a goddess.

"Wow! A hottie Goddess," Zoe said with praise.

Lorca agreed and whistled. Everyone laughed.

Sadows wore a pastel-coloured dress of pink, blue, and purple. It suited her.

"Beautiful," Chandra breathed.

"Amazing!" Lorca said with a smile.

"Absolutely Gorgeous," Zoe spoke.

Zoe hugged Sadows. The day walker clung to the other woman tightly. She was the only link left connected to Zivan and she never wanted to let go.

"Alright, Mon. Time to go out to da club," Chandra said and held Sadows' hand. The vampire who was still a girl at heart smiled.

The girls went to the club. They had drinks and danced the night away. Men were not the only ones that hit on them. There were women that wanted a piece of their action.

Zoe and Lorca took an interest in a couple that were there. The one girl was dark like Chandra and had purple highlights in her afro that was tied back. She was a lithe girl with small bust and a booty that would not quit. Zoe wanted a piece of that ass. Lorca nodded her agreement.

The other girl was a brunette. Wavy hair that reached down to her small tightly shaped butt. She had rather, large pillowy breasts that could be fun to play with.

"You know Zoe, the three of us could make that girl a tasty vanilla swirl between us," Lorca joked.

Zoe laughed and kissed her wife.

"Let's do it with cherries on top," Zoe chuckled.

They went up to the couple to talk about what could be done about having a new relationship for the night.

The couple agreed and were soon on the dance floor with them.

The night went on and Sadows was having fun with her friends. It helped to keep her mind settled for a brief time at least.

With the night almost done, everyone went to Chandra's apartment in the city.

Zoe, Lorca and the two other women went into the bedroom for their fun while Sadows and Chandra laid down on the fold out couch in the living room.

The two women laid there facing each other.

"Will you ever give Sitri a chance?" Sadows asked abruptly.

This caught Chandra off guard. She was not sure what to say.

"I don't know, Cher," Chandra replied.

"Please, Chandra. What if you never get the chance to? What if something happens..." Sadows let her words hang.

Chandra knew what that meant. It has already happened to the day walker. She may never get the chance to tell Zivan the things she wanted to.

Chandra frowned and held Sadows.

"I don't want you to loose an opportunity to love someone like her," Sadows sobbed softly.

"I know, Cher. I love you for your concern," Chandra mused.

Couples Having Fun

Zoe and Lorca were having the time of their lives with the couple they had picked up from the club. There were giggles and laughter. Teasing and moans of pleasure. Even cherries used in foreplay.

Zoe and Lorca have become very accomplished lovers as of late. They had this couple in the throes of passion. Brining them to ecstasy continuously. Both, Zoe, and Lorca had their faces buried in between the thighs of the two women.

Wife and wife switched partners. They kissed each other savoring the flavours.

"She is truly a vanilla swirl delight," Lorca whispered in her wife's ear before muff driving the girl Zoe was with.

Zoe smiled with a glint of mischief. The brunette girl blushed; her cheeks turned bright red.

"Darling, I'm going to make you feel great," Zoe promised as her tongue lashed out and teased the other woman, making her groan deeply.

The woman she was with, her name was Trisha Herd, An accountant with her own business firm. Her dark-skinned partner Tamera Hastens owned a voodoo shop in New Orleans. Now, they were here with two hyper-sexualized women that would make their night a lasting memory never to be *forgotten.*

Soon, Zoe and Lorca found themselves in the same positions those girls were in. They were amazing lovers and brought the Fae women to climaxes repeatedly. They too switched partners. Zoe could not decide which girl she liked best and was grateful for not being able to choose. She wanted both. Then they were both on her. So, pleasurable. Lorca kissed Zoe then worked her way to a breast and sucked hard on a nipple, only heightening the pleasures.

Lorca had been devoured by the two women and Zoe was sucking her wife's nipple. She bit down hard, and Lorca climaxed hard. Her creamy essence flowed out and is licked clean.

Zoe held Lorca's hand and gripped tightly.

"Zoe. It feels wonderful to fuck like this," Lorca panted between breaths.

"I know, my love," Zoe breathed and kiss her wife's chocolate lips.

"We were wondering if and when the both of you were ever in New Orleans again that this relationship could possibly continue?" Trisha suggested.

Tamera had a hopeful look about her. How could Zoe and Lorca say *No*.

Lorca nodded and Zoe smiled warmly.

"Of course, but..." Zoe raised a finger, "we sometimes like to have another partner in the mix. We have a friend you would really enjoy. She will rock your world. Also, we like to have a man in the mix once in awhile. We like the taste of sperm," Zoe finished.

"So, what do you girls say to that?" Lorca asked.

"Deal," Tamera agreed.

"Definitely," Trisha nodded.

"As Chandra would say, 'Laissez les bon temps rouler – Let the good times roll'," Zoe shouted. All the women giggled.

They all made out again and more love making throughout the night.

Meeting the Alpha

Michael landed on the rooftop of a high-rise building. All around him were women with blank expressions. There were witches and may have been werewolves also.
 He felt confident he could make his escape. These humans were beneath him anyway. He was an Immortal, beyond what humans could ever understand.
 Aila walked out in a skirt suit. Rocking her muscled curves like she always did. Her amber eyes glowed. This made the angel uneasy deep down. He could not understand why. This woman was a werewolf. Barely above a human or vamp.
 "For someone who called this meeting you seem to look upon me like I'm some sort of lowly class citizen," the she-wolf smiled viciously.
 Yet Michael was no fool. He could sense great power in her and it made him afraid.
 Aila could smell his fear.
 "You can't defeat me," she said straight up.

Michael scoffed at her. His wings turned into light and a blade of light appeared. He struck out at her.

Aila caught the blade in her hand. Flames roared and burned him. The angel fell back and tried to hold his burnt arms to his chest. He had never felt such pain before.

The she-wolf stood above him. She chuckled. Michael realized that he was not healing. He looked up at the fire-wolf.

"H... how?" he questioned.

This cannot be, he thought with dread. Now, knew why he needed to fear her. He had a bad feeling this was only a fraction of her power.

There is a reason, why I am the Sun Shaman," Aila spoke.

She gripped his chin in her hand. Heat radiated from her in waves. Suddenly, his arms began to heal.

"Wrong me again and I will inflict such wounds that will never heal. You will end up as a mishappen freak that no one shall recognize who or what you are," her voice chilled him to the bone even though she gave off such heat.

Aila moved away to give him room to breath. How had this woman acquired such amazing power?

"My brother Lucy is trapped. I believe you can free him," Michael said with more desperation than intended.

"Oh?" Aila raised her brows.

"He continuously burns to ash and then is resurrected. His mind is mostly gone but he has moments of recognition," Michael explained.

Aila stared at him hard. Her thoughts were dark with speculations.

"Will you trust me enough to examine him?" Aila asked.

Before he could answer, a voice demanded his attention. It was her again. It was a seductive whisper at first.

The angel held his head. The throbbing ache became more insistent. Demanding attention.

Michael flew into the air. Up into the clouds at a speed and height that he was no longer in sight.

Track him," Aila said as she turned and went back inside the building.

Breakfast

The next morning Chandra and Sadows were making breakfast. Potatoes chopped along with red peppers. Butter added with minced garlic. Andouille sausage sliced and fried. Eggs scrabbled tabasco sauce mixed in with Cajun spice.

Sadows shredded pepper jack cheese into the mix.

Zoe and Lorca came out of the bedroom nude as jay birds, along with the other couple Tamera and Trisha, also nude.

The smell of sex permeated from the bedroom strongly. Chandra smiled at the women.

Sadows plugged her nose.

"You all reek like sexy time," she puckered her lips in a weird face.

Everyone giggled.

"True dat, Cher," Chandra threw in.

They started to sit down at the table.

"Food is ready, Mon," Chandra announced.

She served everyone a plate then sat down to eat with them.

"Oh, Chandra. This is so good. Nothing like home cooked Cajun food," Tamera praised.

"Yes, Chandra. Thank you very much. This is delicious," Trisha said and stuffed her face full.

"Oh, hon. This is amazing," Zoe said with a look of yummy taste buds that were in heaven.

"I love it. So, yummy," Lorca had a look of ecstasy on her features.

Zoe giggled. "Great to eat tasty food again, eh?"

Lorca nodded. "Sure is."

"Chandra, you really are a great cook. Please teach me how to make other dishes," Sadows begged.

"I shall, girlie. Thank you all for your praise. I appreciate it," Chandra said with a smile.

When everyone finished, Zoe and Lorca gathered the dishes and went to wash them. The two women stood close to one another and every so often their hips would gently collide.

Tamera and Trish spoke with Chandra and Sadows.

"I own a voodoo shop and the Baron of New Orleans likes to come in every so often," Tamera said.

"He is a perfect gentleman," Trisha said.

"Oh yes, he is. Samedi is Chandra's true love," Sadows said excitedly.

Chandra smiled at her friend's comment. The couple looked at one another in wonderment.

"You are the da voodoo queen of New Orleans?" Tamera asked.

"Truly?" Trisha asked also.

Chandra nodded with a wane shy like smile.

"We should go out tonight and celebrate your return with drinks and dancing, praise Erzulie," Tamera grew excited.

"I'm okay with it if you are, Chandra. I'd like to dance with you again," the day walker said with a smile.

"Awrite, Cher. We do dat," Chandra replied.

"Aw! We are so glad Chandra," Zoe and Lorca said at the same time. They hugged the voodoo queen, then both kissed her cheeks.

The morning filled with friendship, laughter, and love.

Another Night Together

Sitri laid in Samedi's arms. They watched an old movie on an old tube television. The movie was playing from an old VCR machine even. Sitri thought it was the coolest piece of older technology she had seen.

Samedi sent a text on his phone.

"The girls are staying out another night, Cher," Samedi said.

"Is everything alright?" Sitri asked in concern.

"Yes, Cher. It awrite. Zoe and Lorca have met another couple. Tamera and Trisha. I know them. Been to their voodoo shop a couple of times. Seems they are excited to meet their queen and want to hang out," he showed Sitri the text.

"Wow! That is cool! So, we get to spend another night together, alone!" Sitri said with a smile.

"Oh, Cher," Samedi breathed into her mouth.

Their lips met in a longing kiss of passion. A passion heated by a lust demoness' desires and a voodoo Baron's passion for one of the women he loves.

"Oh Samedi. Pump a baby into me," Sitri said breathlessly.

Her panting breath was hot in his ear. He moaned her name. Soon, they were in the throes of passion. Their love making would last on and off throughout the night.

They did manage to finish watching the movie. Rewinding to were they left off was a pain to find and took a bit of time.

"Samedi, I want to have your baby so badly," Sitri confessed her emotions.

"I know, Cher," he replied, "we shall have fun trying."

"I want a child with you more than anything. There is one other thing I want more…" her words did not have a chance to finish as Samedi kissed her.

"I know, Cher. She will come around. I promise. She needs time, still."

Love is all Sitri ever wanted in life. To receive love and to give it.

Girls Night Out

Chandra, Sadows, Zoe, Lorca, Tamera, and Trisha went for a night on the town. Partying. Drinking. Dancing. Girls only!

Wives' Zoe and Lorca danced with the couple Tamera and Trisha. They bumped and grinded to the flow of the music.

"Look at them dance Chandra. It's so, erotic. This song is so damn powerful. Daniel Graves is a genius with his lyrics," Sadows shouted as to be, heard above the music.

Chandra agreed with her day walker friend. Aesthetic Perfection was a great band with great music.

I don't feel myself at all.
As you rise, I slowly fall.
So, I choke, and I ache, on my own jealousy.
No, I will never be happy for you.

The four women ruled the dance floor. All eyes strayed to linger upon their moving forms. Men tried to dance with the girls but politely brushed off. Most got the gist. The ones that tried to push were either warned to back off or the bouncers took them out.

Soon, Chandra and Sadows joined the other women, and the heat went up a couple of degrees. People danced around them getting their own groove on with the other half.

It was sexual pheromones that ruled the club. Couples touching and kissing as they danced.

I know it's self-absorbed.
But I'd like to be, adored.
I know it's fake, but I can't relate.
To the world in the way that you do.

The girls wanted to be watched by all. They desired it, get off on it. Zoe climaxed with Tamera on the dance floor. Both women flushed and panted out their breath. Lorca and Trisha kissed and laughed the night away. Chandra and Sadows bumped hips together with arms raised in the air. Every person in that club fantasized about being with those girls. Who would not? They were sizzling hot and the most desirable women in New Orleans this night.

Another song played. Nightmare from Nyxx. She also did songs with Daniel Graves.

You say I'm crazy and I might be.
But if you only knew.
That there's something inside me.
With its sights set on you.
It's kicking, it's screaming.
You're begging and pleading.
And there's no escape from me.

Everyone moved their hips into each other. Things grew steamy between Lorca and Trisha. Skirts raised as they rubbed up against one another's thighs. These girls did not wear panties. To them the clothing only got in the way of what they wanted. Each other!
    Then another song came on and the energy changed. Became more upbeat. The girls jumped about wildly.

Make them go away.
These twisted thoughts inside my head.
(inside my head)
Take me to a place.
Where I can dance until I'm dead.
(dead, dead)

Die In The Disco, by Night Club.

Sweat and sex.

Scents of horny women that did not hold back on their feelings for one another.

Sadows laughed and was genuinely enjoying herself. There was happiness in being with her friends. At least, for now.

Chandra lost herself in the moment with her friends. There was no one she would rather be with at this time in her life.

As for Zoe and Lorca. They were very fond of this couple and agreed to continue relations with them. The couple were all for it. Tonight, filled with juicier loving and new friendship bonds.

As they all left the club, all watched and desired them. They were followed.

Keena Spies

Keena appeared in a blip of black mist and laid upon a large tree limb, arms under her chin and feet kicked in the air lazily.

"I spy with my little sexy eye, sexy time under the full witch moon, bitches," she whispered to herself.

She reached between her thighs to masturbate because she enjoyed what she saw.

"Oh yes Mikael, fuck that slutty she-wolf," Keena moaned under her breath.

Two fingers went into her vagina. She enjoyed the sticky slapping sound they made. Her eyes rolled in the back of her head.

"Ah! Fuck that dark skinned shaman girl. Make her sing a melody," Keena voice skipped.

Her climax came and she shouted out her glory.

"Oh Fafner, rock my little world," the dark nymph's voice growled. A transformation started. Keena was in the middle of a change when she fell out of the tree. She scraped herself up off the ground. The transformation stopped and the faerie reverted to herself.

"Hello Keena. You cannot be here," a voice spooked her.

"Helga? What are you doing here?" Keena asked confused.

"I'm sorry love, but you can't be here. Your madness is getting out of hand dear friend," Helga said sadly.

"W... what a... are you saying?" Keena questioned.

Fear clutched her heart. Something was off about her shaman friend.

"Know I love you," Helga finished.

A figure with a crown of antlers appeared out of the mist turned purple from the witch moon.

"Daddy? Why are you here?" Keena asked in a too small a voice. Tears began to tumble from her eyes.

"It is time for you to come home, child," another voice said.

The faerie spun around. Her eyes widened. She began to shiver in fright.

"M... M... Mother?" Keena whispered darkly.

A Black maned woman with dark skin walked up to the dark nymph. Eyes black like Keena's glistened with a shine.

"Hello, my daughter," the dark Fey Queen said lightly.

"You can't keep me here," Keena assured them and tried to leave.

"What the fuck? Why..." she paused and looked to Helga.

"I'm sorry, Keena," Helga said with a frown.

Keena rushed to Helga and pleaded with her friend.

"Please, Helga. Don't let her take me away. She is a vile woman. Please save me from her," Keena cried out.

Helga struggled with her own emotions but knew this must happen for the sake of her granddaughter and Mikael. For Sadows and Zivan. For all their friends. Keena must be, contained. She has caused too much trouble as is.

Keena looked franticly to her father.

"Daddy, please. Let your new wives contain me. I know Zoe and Lorca would treat me well and not put up with my shit."

"They are not powerful enough to deal with you, my dear," Tara said sadly.

"New wives?" the Dark Fey Queen questioned in annoyance.

"Yes! Daddy has new brides. They are great. Sex with them is so wonderful," Keena threw in as a bonus defence.

This only infuriated the Fey queen.

"You mated without my permission?" she said angrily. "I am within my right to kill your new Trollip whores."

The Stag Lord gripped the Fey Queen's chin. "You will do as told or I will erase your existence and rewrite it as your worse fear. But you shall retain all your memories so they would haunt you until you die. Then I will rewrite you again as something else you despise yet you remember everything still. I would keep doing it for all eternity. Do you still wish to kill my new lovers?" Tara's voice was a void calm.

It chilled the Fey Queen to her core. She knew if she even thought to hurt those two women, he would do just like he said.

"My apologies, my Prime," the Dark Fey Queen said shaken.

"Daddy always had a way with words," Keena said as she hugged him.

The Blood King hugged his daughter.

"Be well Keena. Stay safe," he said and kissed his daughter's brow.

"Time to go my daughter," the Fey Queen said, and darkness surrounded them. They disappeared.

The Stag Lord turned to Helga.

"Keena will not be held long but hopefully long enough to achieve what needs to be done."

Helga waited. He had more to say.

"My brother is now free. He shall come for you soon, Moon Shaman," he warned. Then he was gone.

Helga smiled. She looked forward to meeting Fafnir again.

Battle

Ladies of the night roamed the streets walking back to Chandra's apartment. Loud party girls laughing and telling jokes. Just having a plain ole fun time.

Sadows had her arm within Chandra's as they walked down the road.

"Chandra. Vamps are following us," Sadows whispered.

"I know, Cher. They followed us from da club," the voodoo queen replied in a low tone.

"We have to protect our new friends," Zoe leaned into Lorca and whispered.

"Of course," Lorca said with a grin.

But the couple were prepared to fight. Green webbing flared to life out of Tamera's hands. The web went toward a building and wrapped around two vamps. They screamed in outraged pain before they burned away to charred lumps.

Trisha had a pistol in her hands that she took out of her purse. Silver bullets killing another vamp. The couple were a good team just like Zoe and Lorca.

Zoe ran past the couple with flaming arms and turned more vamps to ash. Lorca clawed her way through vamps. Their bodies fell in dried husks.

Chandra spread her green flames behind them and burned vamps to charred husks.

A vamp grabbed Sadows from behind. She just stood there. He gripped her breasts and his reeking breath upon her neck discussed her.

"My mistress sends her regards. Says that I can take you any way I choose. She says Zivan is safe in her ever-loving care," then the vamp bit into Sadows neck and drank his fill.

She was numb at first by his words. She let the vamp drink knowing full well what would happen to him.

NOT WITHOUT MY CONSENT!

The vamp pulled away in a panic. He stared at his hands and watched as the blood in his veins turned a bright red. Sadows' gaze turned red. Eyes of bloody rage were a storm of fury.

"Where is my Zivan?" she demanded.

"I... I don't know. He is a prisoner of my mistress," the vamp stuttered out.

"Where is she?" Sadows ordered.

"Vancouver!" he stated. He tried to resist the day walker but felt compelled to answer her. He enjoyed answering her. Felt freeing.

"All you other vamps. Come feed on your friend here," Sadows commanded.

The other vampires went and piled upon their comrade to feed. They began to twist in agony. Their screeches filled the night. The vamp that fed from Sadows began to expand until he exploded. Then all the other vampires exploded into pieces that soon melted into a sludge like substance.

"Bos Moi, girlie," Chandra swore.

The other women were in awe of the day walker. Sadows stood there. A melancholy suddenly overwhelmed her. She fell to her knees and sobbed.

"Zivan!" she cried out.

Zoe ran to her and hugged her friend, her sister.

"We will find him, alive," Zoe promised.

"She is doing horrible things to him," Sadows choked out.

"Please don't think that!" Zoe cried herself.

The two women held onto one another in the middle of the roadway.

Little Spy

He was invisible. A small creature that could not be sensed. His movements were not heard. His motions could not be felt as he sat upon her shoulder. Nor could you smell him. He had no scent.

The imp was still and observant. Took in his surroundings. Waited for an opportunity to make his move.

The woman walked in a casual manner into a building. It was loud and full of people. Music blared. An announcer spoke into a microphone. It was the DJ.

"...And by popular demand. Closer by NIN, my bitches."

The crowd went wild, and the dancing grew more energetic. Screams of girls shouted obscene words. Boys gyrating like they were humping. The perverseness of the young.

You let me violate you.
You let me desecrate you.
You let me penetrate you.
You let me complicate you.

These words suited the woman who walked through the club. She grinned at the lyrics of the song. A fingernail picked between a fang.

(Help me)
I broke apart my insides.
(Help me)
I've got no soul to sell.
(Help me)
The only thing that works for me.
Help me get away from myself.

The woman laughed. It was a horrible fit of laughter. Then calmed to a giggle that came off dark. The imp was afraid. This creature was a nasty piece of work.

She was in the basement and the music sounded like a thudding drum. Then she entered a room where a boy was bound. The imp leaped into the air and flew up onto the light fixture on the ceiling. It watched how the woman smiled. The glint in her eye.

"Momma has come home to play," she chuckled darkly as her clothes fell to the floor. She went on top of the table to be with the boy.

The imp watched for a moment more before flying out of the room. He would report back to his mistress the location.

Fear

It was a warped vision. Sights wavered and shifted about in an uneven manner. A wobble effect put strain on the eyes. A migraine throbbed steadily in her head. The pain grew agonizing slow. It creeped to every part of the head. It moved and writhed like a parasite seeking its prey.

The world seemed tilted and moved in awkward angles. She felt off balance by this and staggered about like a mindless drunkard. Her stomach heaved and she threw up.

She wiped her mouth with the back of a hand and walked away. She felt terrible. Sick. Weakened.

There he suddenly was. Her man. The love of her life. One true mate.

"Zivan! How I've miss you my love," Sadows said happily.

She hugged him close to her. All those ailments forgotten. There was only him. his scent... he smelt strange.

She looked at his features. He smiled. Fangs glinted in the light. Horror reeled into the day walker's mind.

"No!" she breathed, "it can't be." Disbelief filled her. Reality came crashing down upon her as the silver-eyed vamp came into view.

"Hello, my love," Zivan said to the other woman and kissed her deeply.

Aaruhi laughed in delight. Her eyes flashed. She moved with such speed, faster than Sadows' eye could see. Aaruhi and Zivan were upon the day walker. Their fangs sank into her. They drank. Sadows panicked. She felt her life drain away. Darkness closed in as her eyelids became heavy...

Sadows awoke screaming. Blood tendrils slashed about and tore the bed to ribbons. Chandra ducked down upon the floor.

"Bos Moi, girlie. Calm your shit down, Mon," the voodoo queen shouted.

Zoe burst into the room and hugged the girl.

"Easy Sister. I'm here for you. We are all here for you. We love you. We will find Zivan," Zoe began to cry.

Sadows held onto Zoe like her life depended on it. Both women sobbed together.

Lorca came in and hugged both her wife and the day walker. Tears were in her eyes.

"Stay with her, my love," Lorca said and kissed Zoe's mouth softly, then kissed Sadows' forehead.

Sadows squeezed Lorca's hand in thanks. Lorca went back into the bedroom with Tamera and Trisha. She explained the events that happened.

Things calmed down. Sadows went back to sleep with Zoe and Chandra in her arms. She would be safe. Secure. Loneliness gone for the night. No more fear.

The Mission

In a cargo plane with weapons and gear that made this team sexy as all hell. Everyone did their final checks before going into battle. These were hardened warriors. Only humans but tough as they come.
"Alright people, we will be landing E.T.A. nine hundred hours," Lucile shouted. "We move and we kill everything. I want my son back unharmed, and I want that vamp bitch a pile of ash." Her hard stare said there was no room for mistakes and the consequences of failure would be costly.
Brock blew a bubble. It popped and he chewed.
"She is one bad ass chick, man. She scares the fuck out of me," he said seriously.
Stacy giggled. The others looked to one another with offset smiles. They never thought he would have said such a thing before. This guy was fearless.

"Hey Hon. Can I have some?" Stacy asked as her lips met Brocks. Her tongue explored his mouth and made a dash for his chewing gum. He gave it up to her without a fight. She pulled away chewing her victory.

"Mm! Tastes so… much better this way," she exclaimed as if she just tasted the best food ever.

"That's gross," Chan said. His almond shaped eyes glared.

"You don't have bubble gum in Japan?" Stacy asked playfully as she twirled gum around a finger.

There were chuckles. Chan scratched the side of his face with a middle finger.

Everyone laughed. Even the stone-faced Yu Sama smiled.

Brock pulled out a pack of gum and offered it to his teammates. They each took a piece.

"We are here to kick ass and chew bubble gum, my bitches," Brock declared.

"Bite the bullet," everyone said as a chorus.

"You two have been more of a pain in the ass since getting together," Jax said and flexed his ebony arms.

"Only to annoy you Jackie boy," Brock laughed.

Jax laughed with his teammates.

"I bet you cracker Hispanic," Jax threw back.

Brock chuckled.

They landed and they got into SUV's and drove to the destination. An abandoned building complexes. They went in hot. Guns blazing and vamps dying. When their sweeps were finished there was still no sign of Zivan.

Lucile had a vamp chained in silver.

"Where is Zivan, my son," she yelled.

The vamp screeched in denial. She put its hand in sunlight and held it there until it disintegrated into ash.

The vamp never spoke and died without revealing anything relating to him. Lucile let the sun take him.

"Another dead end," Malcom said.

He hugged his wife. She snuggled into her husband and sobbed quietly.

Dark Queen

Darken woods. Trees of black bark. Silver leaves that gave off a soft glow. Shadows leaped everywhere ready and waiting to pounce.

Creatures of the Fey roamed here. This was the lands of the dark Fey Queen. Keena was home with her mother and none too happy about it.

The Queen knew her daughter well. Knew of the madness that afflicted her. The dark nymph was dangerous to herself and everyone around her. The bitch was too powerful for her own good. Ever since she...

"Mother," Keena said with contempt, "why am I here?"

The queen mother smirked. She had plans for her daughter.

"Are you mad at me for killing my brother. He was your valued son after, all," Keena mocked.

"You know damn well he was a piece of shit and I do not care in the least about him. Although, you better not bear a child because of your actions. You sick twisted little nymph," the Queen glared.

    The Dark Fey Queen gripped Keena's chin painfully.

    "You shall do as told, child. I have a mission for you. If you disobey me, I will rip the baby factory from your womb, and you shall never bear children ever again. You will never mate that lover you so adore," she finished and kissed her daughter lightly on the lips.

    Keena frowned as she continued to follow her mother deeper into the dark Fey kingdom. Fear clutched her heart and squeezed its dreadfulness within. The dark nymph shivered involuntarily.

    They came to a throne made up of a twisted tree of bones and thorns. The Dark Fey Queen sat upon her throne with a dark nasty smirk.

    "You remember Kreale," she pointed to a massive Fae with thorns down his spine. Large muscles shaped the giant creature. Between his legs was a massive penis that had needles along the head like a crown.

    Keena's eyes widened. She had this dreadful feeling something bad was about to happen.

    "Take her. Do not be gentle," the Queen laughed darkly.

"No!" Keena screamed. "Mother please. Don't do this. He is too big for me. I'll bleed out," Keena sobbed.

"That is the point my dear. Kreale fucks me all the time and I never have any problems. He satisfies me simply fine," the Dark Fey Queen chuckled and spread her legs to rub herself while her lover raped her daughter.

The Dark Fey Queen had more than a twisted sense of humour. She was just downright vile. She enjoyed the screams of pain from her daughter. It got her off as she moaned her dark pleasure.

Back in the Bayou

Chandra brought the girls back to her Bayou home. Even brought Tamera and Trisha along. Fellow vamp killers have more than proven themselves as friends. Chandra liked the couple. They were good people. They were fond of Zoe and Lorca. Chandra was sure those feelings would deepen.

The voodoo queen's thoughts strayed. Her thoughts were about Samedi and Sitri. Could their relationships also deepen? Chandra was not so sure about that. Would her prejudices allow her to have feelings for the demoness?

They pulled up to the dock and Chandra turned off the motor. Samedi and Sitri were there waiting. Sitri caught Chandra's eye and smiled.

Chandra smiled back. It was weak but there and she meant it. Sitri greeted her.

"You are alright my Queen," Sitri asked. One knew she was uncomfortable with how she spoke her words. Could tell the demoness wanted to say something on the more intimate side.

Samedi put his hand on Sitri's shoulder, and she felt comfort from that.

"Hey, Cher," he said to his queen.

"Samedi," Chandra breathed and kissed him. Sitri's eyes lit up. She yearned to be in between them.

How I want to be their creamy filling, the demoness thought and bit her lip.

This did not go unnoticed. Lorca introduced the couple to Sitri.

"This is Sitri, the girl we told you about," Lorca bragged.

"Oh," said Trisha with wide bright eyes.

"Pleased to meet you," Tamera said excitedly.

"Hi," Sitri said in confusion.

Sadows gripped her hand and pulled her away. "I need to talk to you, Sitri."

They went into the house and then into Grandma Chandra's room. They laid on the bed together facing each other.

"I want to go back to Toronto. The same way I was, brought here. With you and I in the coffin again. I'll feel safer that way," Sadows said.

"Okay, sweetie. We will tell the others. Is tomorrow alright?" Sitri asked.

Sadows nodded and cuddled into her friend. The lust demon held the day walker in her arms.

She loved her friend on such a deep level that it felt good not having those sexual desires for her.

As for those two women she met on the other hand, Sitri wanted a piece of that action. She smiled and soon fell asleep. Dreams of a couple that explored every inch of her.

Oni Thoughts

Oni awoke and stood looking out the condominium window of Lacy's bedroom. She liked it here. Liked being in this city. Toronto. It had a glorious tower. Made this city unique even though other cities had towers. Not like this one.

She sighed as she touched the glass with her fingertips. The lights down below were like stars. Who would have thought that any kind of city would one day light up the sky!

Strong muscled arms wrapped around her waist and the silver-eyed samurai leaned in those arms. She enjoyed the comfort it brought her. Lips met the nape of her neck and she moaned softly.

"Penny for your thoughts," he said huskily.

"I like her, a lot," Oni said.

"I'm happy," he said back.

"I hope she likes me."

"She does!"

Oni enjoyed the other woman. Sex was great with her and the emotions the samurai felt were genuine.

"Hey you two. Come back to bed. I'm lonely," Lacy said with a pout.

Oni smiled and kissed her man.

"Should we sandwich her?" Oni asked.

"Good idea. Let's do it," he answered.

They went back to bed and cuddled themselves back to sleep.

Brock and Stacy

Brock held his girl close, and she enjoyed his touch upon her flesh. They were in a hotel in the city of Vancouver. The team is on rest time. That and Malcom and Lucile need time together. Their son was missing perchance dead or turned. The couple have not spent any time together.

Brock did not think he could spend time away from Stacy. Even when they were not a couple, they had spent most, of their time together. He cannot remember when he first started to fall in love with Stacy. Perhaps, always has been.

Stacy on the other hand, had an instant attraction to Brock. Fell, hard, and fast. When introduced and they fist bumped there was electricity between them, and she was, hooked. They just clicked and have been friends ever since.

Brock squeezed arms around Stacy, and she raised her hand to his cheek, their lips met in a kiss that lasted a long time.

"I love you so much, Stacy," Brock murmured.

"Oh, baby. How I love you," Stacy breathed back.

"Stacy. I don't know if I want to do this job anymore. I just want us to fuck like minx and make babies," he said seriously with a passion in his voice that she had never heard before.

She looked at him stunned. When she read into his eyes, they were pleading with her.

"Sounds great to me. I'm down love," she replied truthfully.

She wanted a family. Children running around the house. Her man in her arms.

"Make love to me, Brock. Let's make babies," Stacy breathed.

Brock responded with a groan. He kissed his girl with a heated passion that made her gasp in pleasure. Their love making began into the night. Brock would treat his girl with a loving care that she desired and craved.

Malcom and Lucile

Malcom held his wife in his arms. She cried freely. Something she has not done in years. Her emotions were always in check, in control, channelled.

Malcom marveled how his wife could compartmentalize everything. He came off as a hard angry asshole. Which he was, especially toward his children. He let out a sigh of regret.

Lucile looked at him with tear-streaked cheeks.

"Malcom. Make love to me. I need to feel something, anything," she pleaded and dragged him on top of her.

Lucile kissed her husband continuously.

"I need you inside me, baby. Fuck me please! I need you. Love me," she kept breathing her words into his mouth.

Malcom could never deny anything to his wife. He slid into her easily and quickly. He had not expected her to be wet as she was. He half expected her to be dry. Not truly into it. Wanted to hurt more to feel something, anything. He thought she wanted tender sex. He was wrong? No. She bucked her hips against him as a sign that she wanted it hard, and fast.

Their love making was fast beat and ended quickly. It did not take Lucile long to have an orgasm. Malcom made only a couple of thrusts when she suddenly screamed out her pleasure.

"Oh, it has been too long, baby."

Malcom groaned. He was on the verge of ejaculation.

"Yes! Squirt it all inside me," Lucile begged.

Soon as he came, she had another orgasm. Her legs locked around his waist tightly. Her arms brought him closer to her.

"I want us to stay like this for the night," she murmured in his ear.

Malcom relaxed his weight against her. He still throbbed inside her. She moaned softly as she fell asleep with a smile.

"I love you, Lucile," he whispered in her ear.

"I love you too," she groaned back sleepily.

Malcom loved his wife with every fiber of his body. He hated being separated from her. He always had separation anxiety when apart. To be with her now made him feel at home. Safe!

Hunter

He was still seeking out his prey. The one that imprisoned him in the bog. This monster craved her on a deep level that pertained to all consuming madness.

Hunger.

A dark desire to feed on the enemy. This creature knew nothing else but that hatred for the dark nymph. Her betrayal will cost everything that she ever loves. The bog monster will eat her and her friends and family.

Soon he will be able to travel in a blink of an eye, just as she does. He just needed to eat more souls. Humans were a delicious treat indeed, but faeries and other Fae tasted far better.

There just so happened to be something to eat now. A child played with a doll. She sat upon a rock.

It was easy to gobble the child up in a single bite. She did not even cry out as he chewed vigorously.

Without a second thought the dark Fey creature moved on. Not a care that this child had a family that would miss her. Its thought was only on revenge upon the dark nymph.

I am coming for you Keena, you dark hearted bitch. I will devour you.

Recon

Yu and Chan were on a recon mission. They decided it was time to find the real hideout and both dressed to the hilt.

Chan wore a black suit that made his features sharp and handsome looking. His slight build filled the clothing to a nice snug fit. He was rocking the suit. His jet-black hair combed neat and smooth.

Yu on the other hand wore a maroon slip dress that revealed a slim toned leg. High heeled stilettos gave her extra height. Make-up applied light and even. Dark red lip stick graced her small thick lips.

Chan could not help but admire her.

"You look ravishing," he breathed.

She gave a half smirk.

"Why thank you, good sir," she said politely. "Will you dance with me?" she then asked.

Chan only nodded. He only had eyes for her.

Concentrate on the mission, Chan, he thought to himself.

They went onto the dance floor. Bodies swayed and bumped and grinded. The energy was high and upbeat. People groped each other and the sexual energy was so high it was a red flashing light that said, 'I'm ready for action.'

"I see her!" Yu stated and swayed her body around so Chan could follow her line of sight. He saw the silver-eyed vamp. He made sure only to glance in her direction and not make eye contact. Chan smiled down at Yu. Good thing they brought their comms. Made it easier to communicate in this environment of loud music and not heard by prying ears.

"Come on," Yu said and took Chan by the hand. They followed the vamp bitch down a hall, and they went into the women's washroom, but noticed that she went down a set of stairs.

Yu giggled and then kissed Chan on the mouth. He went with it. They kissed, stealing more moments.

"Someone likes to be kissed by a Chinese woman," she said and leaned into Chan. He groaned softly.

"No. just by you," Chan admitted red faced.

He is so attracted to Yu and has been for a while now.

They left the club and went back to the hotel. They went into her room.

They kissed and started to undress.

"This is only sex, right? Or... do you want something more?" She questioned.

Chan smiled. Yu loved that smile. It gripped her and made her body tingle.

"I'd like to see if this goes further myself," he revealed.

Yu grabbed him and he fell on top of her. She moaned. Yu needed this right now. So did Chan. Sex, has a way to relief stress. This night would be good for them, and they would reveal their findings to Malcom and Lucile in the morning.

The Evil That Women Do

"Do not clean yourself off, my dear. Keep all that gore on your wonderful penis. Fuck your queen. Please me with your prowess," the Dark Fey Queen commanded.

The dark Fey creature did as, told. He pumped his prowess into the Dark Fey Queen. She was a perverse whore who enjoyed pain and torment.

"Oh, my wonderful monster. Impregnate your Queen," she sneered.

She grabbed his pointed ear and hissed harshly.

"Do it now or I will slit your throat," she commanded with a growl to her voice.

He released inside her. A deep hallowed groan escaped his jaws. The Queen kissed his forehead.

"You have satisfied me well, my brute. Now, go rape my daughter again. Teach her the error of her ways. I shall return shortly. Then you can have your way with me again," she promised with a vile grin.

    She stood then ran her finger along the dark Fey's jawline. She walked down from her throne. Breasts bounced purposeful. Her ass brushed against him, and the monster Fey became aroused. The Queen smiled.

    "You are most precious to me!" she stated.

    She waved her hand and walked away. The dark Fey creature watched until she disappeared. He took his time walking away. His queen would be awhile. Gave plenty of time with the daughter.

Dark Nymph

Excruciating agony. That is what Keena felt as she laid in a pool of her own blood and piss. She was healing well, considering the state she was in.

That monster. The way he had ravaged her brought unspeakable pain within her body. He had torn her right open. She had spilt apart. He had reveled in her screams. It had made him enjoy her suffering even more. Her entrails had even hung out from her once beautiful privates. Now, she was a gory mess. A shell of her former self.

Her mother's sick pet Rinekore, the type of demon faerie hybrid that he was, had ripped out her precious wings. The dark nymph sobbed. Tears mixed in with the pool of gore.

A mother is supposed to protect her children, not abuse them.

How dare she!

Keena's anger sparked and would grow in time. For now, she cried.

I want my Daddy!

"Daddy!" she managed to whimper out weakly.

A soft glow appeared. A crown of antlers was, seen in the darkness. Silver fur and eyes glowed with a gentleness that caressed Keena. Held her. Cradled in strong arms of love.

My daughter. I'm so sorry this happened to you. I give you this gift. It shall empower you. The time will come to use it and you shall be who you are meant to be!

His voice soothed Keena into a lull like sleep. A drop of her father's blood dripped into her mouth. A change began. She felt energized. Whole. *Healed.*

Then the Stag Lord was gone as if he has never been. Keena was once again alone. Afraid.

Kreale came. He boasted all his manly glory. Twisted, mangled huge muscles bumped all over his body. This giant planned to take her once more. His massive member was stiff with anticipation. Hard and ready to impale the dark nymph a second time. A gruntled laughter issued from his throat.

"I will enjoy goring you apart again," he said darkly. He stepped forward.

Then a dark void of nothingness came and enveloped everything.

An Offer

They landed in Toronto. The coffin brought out to the Flatiron apartments and placed inside.

Sadows gave Sitri a kiss on the cheek as thanks for traveling with her. The coffin opened and the faces of their friends smiled upon them.

Chandra helped Sitri out. They gazed at one another briefly. Chandra averted her eyes and looked down at Sadows.

"Come Cher. I help you out," Chandra offered her hand.

Sadows hugged the voodoo queen.

"The two of you should just kiss already," Sadows hissed a whisper.

Chandra turned red in embarrassment. Samedi patted her back. Chandra kissed him deeply. When she broke away, she pushed the voodoo Baron toward Sitri.

"Hey Samedi," Sitri said happily, and they kissed. "Mm! You taste like Chandra," the lust demon said huskily.

Samedi chuckled and hugged his demoness lover.

"You like it, Cher," he whispered in her ear.

"I'm wet as fuck," she whispered back.

"Have to do something about dat," he laughed.

Him and Sitri went into a bedroom.

"We know what's happening in there," Zoe commented with a smile.

"What's on your mind, Sadows?" Lorca asked.

"I want to talk to Shuzo and Himari," Sadows explained.

"Okay, hon," Zoe said.

Chandra went into the bedroom to let Samedi and Sitri know where they were going. She opened the door slowly. The demoness was crying.

"I'm sorry Samedi. I'm horny but sad. I wish Chandra would… I don't know. I'm so in love with her and I don't understand how to… does she even understand how she feels? Is she confused? She just can't be with me because she only likes men?" Sitri opened herself up.

Chandra lightly tapped the door before opening it further.

"We are going to the Ice Condos to talk to our vampire friends there. Just wanted to let you know. Is everything alright?" Chandra asked.

Sitri had her back to the voodoo queen.

"Everything fine, Cher. You go," Samedi replied.

Chandra nodded. She walked to the bed and hugged Sitri and gripped a breast in her hand. She squeezed gently.

"You take care of our man. Protect him wit your life, Cher," Chandra breathed heavily. The voodoo queen still was not sure if she would be into a woman, but the thought occurred to her in this moment. She just could not bring herself to do it yet.

She then left the room abruptly. Sitri still had tears. This time they were of happiness.

The girls left the apartments and went to visit their vampire friends.

Sadows knocked on the door. It was nightfall.

Shuzo answered. He was surprised.

"Come in," he spoke.

Everyone went inside.

"I have an offer to make, but it is dangerous, and you may not survive," Sadows put out.

Everyone was silent a moment. Then Himari spoke.

"It has to do with drinking your blood, correct?" she asked.

"Yes!" Sadows replied.

"Hon, we have seen what happens when other vamps have tried," Zoe spoke softly in concern.

"I know," Sadows whined.

"It could still work. Maybe when she allowed Bathory to feed it just gave her a peaceful death. Shuzo and Himari, it could do something different," Lorca stressed in the day walker's favour.

"I will try it," Himari said.

"I will try also," Shuzo said.

They both bowed.

Everyone gathered in the couple's bedroom. They both laid down on the bed. Sadows crawled between them and held her wrists out to them.

"I give you permission to feed," the day walker assured with hopefulness in her eyes.

Both vamps drank. Just a mouthful. A look of ecstasy overcame them. The couple held hands and gazed at one another. They smiled and cuddled into each other. Their eyes closed and...

"NO!" Sadows cried out. Tears filled her eyes.

Chandra checked them. She could not feel a pulse or any signs of life. the voodoo queen closed her eyes and concentrated. Her senses reached out to the vamp couple.

"Sadows. They are alive. They, seem to be hibernating. Maybe going through a sort of change," Chandra made her best guess.

Sadows felt relieved her friends were alive.

"All we have to do is wait then," Sadows said. "If they don't wake tomorrow then all we can do is check up on them every day until they do."

There were nods of agreements all around. So, they waited.

Time to Go

Sadows and the girls were in her apartment in Ice Condos. All fixed up. Not bad for a couple of weeks.

It has been days now and the Japanese vampire couple were still out cold.

The day walker was getting fidgety. She needed to do something. Ready to fight.

"I want my man back!" Sadows said with determination.

"You, sure, Cher?" Chandra asked in concern.

Sadows nodded. She gave a wave with her arm for her friends to follow her. They left the apartment. Into the elevator they went. Girl trip.

Chandra held the door open.

"Wait! Sitri. Tell Samedi we are leaving, please," the voodoo queen asked.

The demoness nodded and left. Went into the other apartment. Moments later she came back out.

"He wants me to give you something," Sitri said awkwardly.

The demoness gently pressed her lips against Chandra's. There was energy there. He had done something. Used his voodoo magic. Sitri pulled away breathless. Chandra could taste her man upon those lush thick lips. The voodoo queen's body tingled. What had he done? Chandra wondered.

They all ended up in the underground parking lot.

Chandra leaned against the coolness of the concrete wall. All flushed and heated she let out a soft moan.

"Chandra!" Sitri yelled and went to her voudon queen.

Lorca and Zoe snickered, trying to hold back their laughter.

"It's not funny," Sitri said worriedly.

Chandra fell to the ground and the demoness hovered above her mistress.

"Chandra. What is wrong?" the lust demon asked urgently.

"Bos Moi, girlie. Your touch..." she never finished her sentence.

Sitri was on top of Chandra. The demoness began to panic.

"What do I do?" Sitri asked.

Sadows raised her brows. Lorca and Zoe were in full laughter. Sitri put off by their behavior grew more concerned for the voodoo queen.

"Get her off!" Sadows stated.

"Put your hands down her pants and rub the hell out of her," Zoe threw in.

Sitri gently placed her hand within Chandra's jeans and rubbed the woman's clit. Instantly the voodoo queen had an orgasm. She shivered and went still.

"You can get off me now," Chandra grated in embarrassment.

The voodoo priestess stood up and did her best to regain her dignity.

Sitri licked her fingers and Chandra gave a look of disgust. The voodoo queen turned away; red faced.

Sitri enjoyed her treat without shame. Everyone burst out laughing.

"Samedi is going to get my foot in his ass, Mon," Chandra threatened.

"Agreed! He needs to be, spanked. I'll do it," Sitri said with a grin.

Chandra slapped her head.

"Bos Moi, girlie. Shut up," Chandra half laughed and was half serious.

"Is everything alright, now?" Sadows asked.

Chandra nodded. She took deep breaths to steady herself.

"Are you sure, Chandra?" Sitri asked in concern.

The voodoo priestess gripped the demoness' cheeks with her hand. The dark-skinned woman kissed the lust demon's lips.

"Will that shut you up about it, Cher," Chandra spoke hotly.

Sitri nodded her compliance.

They followed the day walker to where Zivan's bike was. Sadows mounted the Harley. She leaned on the handlebars and hugged them lovingly.

"Time to get rides and take a road trip to find my man. I so swear to find you my love," Sadows said as blood dripped from her hand.

She had made her blood oath. A vow that would be, *honoured*.

"Ladies. We ride!"

Loss

Darkness reigned here to a degree. The Dark Fey Queen had light within her. She was not an evil creature. Just a woman scorned and full of rage.

Tivy wished she were the one and only mate of the Stag Lord. He was Lord of all Fae creatures. He had mated her sister the faerie queen. Even though she was his first mate Tivy still hated her sister for it. The Dark Fey Queen has always wanted him for herself. Now, he had mated two other women. It sickened her to no end. She must find a way to do away with their existence. She would find a way.

She roamed her domain to find a little bit of solace. To calm her demeanor. She loved the night. Calm yet had a hidden restlessness to it. Quiet. Until a predator caught its prey, then it would go still once again.

The path she walked was one only she traveled. It was a hidden magical pathway were there would be none to disturb her. Helped to collect her thoughts and make dark plans, for the future.

She was so wrapped up in her owns thoughts that she did not notice something was off at first. Tivy suddenly stood still and listened. Sounded like... *Windchimes?*

The Dark Fey Queen gazed up into the trees and saw dark faeries hung with their entrails dangling. Her eyes went wide with rage.

That fool went on a killing spree again, she thought. She would have to teach him a lesson, again!

She stomped her way to her throne and the sight shocked her.

"What the... Fuck!" she uttered.

On the seat of the throne lay Kreale's head. There was something in his mouth that seemed familiar. Tivy gasped. It was his enormous cock that she loved so much.

The appendage fell out and the mouth began to move.

"Hello, Mother!" It was Keena's voice that spoke. "This is my gift to you for all that you have done for me. I have taken that which is most precious to you. May the faerie's light guide you into the Otherworld you, fucking heartless bitch!" Then all was silent. Tivy stood there with her fists clenched. Rage built up inside.

"Keena, you cunt. I will make you pay, Daughter," the Dark Fey Queen roared out. Her outrage was so great that her very realm shook and groaned in anger.

"I swear to do unimaginable things to you. You, fucking whore," Tivy promised darkly.

Tears streaked the Dark Fey Queen's eyes. She crouched down and cradled her lover's cock in her arms. Her sobs were heard for weeks.

To Awaken At Last

Shuzo groaned as he opened his eyes to a room full of daylight. He held his hand up in confusion. Why was it so bright? It took time for his eyes to focus. Then he stared in shock out the bedroom window. He bathed in sunlight. He was fine. Alive!

Himari sat up and moaned softly. She felt tired. She cuddled into her husband's back.

"Why is it so bright in here?" she questioned. Her eyes hurt from the brightness. Then sprang open as she too looked outside into the sunlight.

"We are alive and not on fire. How?" she asked in surprise.

They could feel the heat of the sun. It felt, *nice*. Warming. The couple hugged. They smiled upon one another and kissed gently. Himari leaned her head on Shuzo's shoulder.

"She saved us. We are free to wander the daylight hours now. Wonder if we would be able to eat normal foods?" Shuzo asked.

"Only one way to find out, my husband," Himari said.

"Indeed!" a voice interrupted.

The couple jumped and looked across the room. A woman sat in a chair. She was a strikingly beautiful woman. They knew she was a vampire. She was able to walk in the daylight also. She wore a black dress skirt. It only covered half her thighs and allowed a bountiful amount of her cleavage to hang out. Long thick wavy dark hair draped over a shoulder. She wore a wide brimmed black hat and sunglasses.

"Lady Bathory at your service. Charmed I'm sure," she mocked playfully.

The couple stared at the woman.

"As in the Countess Bathory?" Himari asked in skepticism.

"The one and only, my dears," she said and displayed her arms out in dramatic fashion.

The Countess stood with hands placed on her hips.

"So, are you two ready to go help our girl, Sadows?" she said and gazed at them over her sunglasses with a glint in her eye, fangs bared in a nasty smile.

Another Author's Note

Here we go everyone. I have something to say.
While talking to **Jay Crudge** about a chapter with Keena in it.
"Bitch Must Burn!" His words.
Love yah man! Lol!
So, I instantly produced an idea that may have worked in the chapter, but oh well. I'll just write it here and see what people think.
It will take place after the Dark Fey Queen sees her lover's head on her throne, but no cock in mouth.
So, let me know what you think at:

https://derangedprophet66.wixsite.com/derangedprophet
https://www.patreon.com/Kiltron
derangedprophet66@gmail.com
https://www.facebook.com/kiltron
https://twitter.com/Kiltromakon
https://www.instagram.com/derangedprophet
https://www.deviantart.com/kiltromakon

She saw her precious monster lover's head upon her magnificent throne. Her foots falls scraped in the path. Her movements were slow, lethargic.

Tivy lifted his head off the seat of her throne and caressed it. A sound caught her attention and the Dark Fey Queen glanced over to one side.

A campfire?

There was Keena. Roasting the massive cock that Tivy found most precious to her.

"Hello, Mother! Hungry? We are having roasted sausage," Keena laughed with malice.

"Keena!" Tivy roared. "I will destroy you for this."

The Dark Fey Queen's power erupted, and her domain roared in anger. An upheaval happened, but Keena was nowhere to be, found.

Continued in
Crimson Prophecies
Crypt 6
Sanguine Slave

Paperback & Digital versions

Hardcover version